THE EYE OF THE ELEPHANT

Pam Barnes

Published by: Mapsenrab Publishers
Email: pam.barnes37@gmail.com

ISBN: 978-0-473-41926-4

Cover: Richard Knot

Printed by: Createspace

Introduction

In 1820, around 4,000 British men, women and children set sail from Southampton in 26 ships, successfully passing through the Cape of Storms and landing in Algoa Bay, on the southern coast of the African continent. They were known as the "1820 Settlers". After a few bad years, it was accepted that the African soil and weather made crop farming unproductive. Thus, land sizes were increased and sheep and cattle brought in. Now the Settlers thrived, although dangers lay in defending their patch against indigenous people disputing possession and wild animals in search of sustenance.

Most of these Settlers stayed close to Algoa Bay, but some moved inland. A group eventually settled in an area in the lee of the Drakensberg Mountains, called East Griqualand. Because they clung to their British heritage, they were known as the "gentlemen farmers".

Although the characters in this novel are fictional, I have tried to remain true to the era.

This is Algie's story. A descendent of these settlers, growing up on a dairy farm in East Griqualand, he runs away under a cloud of misunderstanding from the family and farm he loves. It takes an unexpected meeting in a most unlikely place to give him the courage to go home.

He reminds me of my father.

Pam Barnes

Contents

Chapter 1

There is a range of mountains, some distance inland from the sea, which forms a 1,000-mile last-quarter, moon-shaped barricade around the south-eastern corner of Southern Africa. It is known by several names. One is Quathlamba (piled up rocks). Another is "Barrier of Spears". But it is the third name "Drakensberg" (Dragon Mountain) which would be written into the maps of South Africa that were to come. The range rises in dramatic peaks, some over 11,000 feet above sea level, dips down in seemingly benign gorges to taunt the traveler with the promise of a pathway, and has an amphitheater of such magnitude that even herds of dinosaurs would have been as dwarfs had they gathered in its encircling arms.

If the Drakensberg had been fashioned by its Maker to deter foes from acts of aggression or curtail heroic endeavours, it has failed on both counts. Many wars were fought in its ambience – local tribal wars, Settlers against indigenous tribes, Boer against the British Empire. And its seemingly impenetrable heights were conquered by warriors on foot and riders on horseback. And wagons loaded with people and supplies – dragged up and over by every painful step of the great hump-shouldered, long horned Afrikander oxen, as the Settlers clawed their way inland looking for fertile land on which to establish their farms.

In the year 1820, around 4,000 intrepid British men, women and children set sail upon the oceans in 26 brave-hearted wooden sailing ships, successfully passing through the Cape of Storms and landing in Algoa Bay, on the southern coast of the great African continent. They were known as the "1820 Settlers". The Britain they left behind was economically depressed and politically turbulent. This new land, painted in such glowing terms by Governor Lord Charles Somerset, promised a better life. Some sources record that each settler family was given free passage, seed and implements – and a tent – and allocated a patch of land, with repayment only expected after the first harvest. Two conditions were imposed. It was forbidden to own slaves or hire the indigenous people as workers, and they were only allowed to farm on their allocated land.

Very soon many of these Settlers regretted their decision to come to this country! The inhospitable veld (as the flat open country was called), dense scrub and rocky nature of the soil, so unlike the verdant pastures they had left behind, made cultivation virtually impossible. Incursions by marauding hostile tribes (mainly Xhosas) were a constant threat, and some Settlers lost their lives in defense of their unproductive piece of earth. The grain and vegetables they managed to grow fell prey to locusts, browsing game and droughts. After the first four years of backbreaking toil, came the floods, and washed away even the few inches of hard-won progress. Financial ruin and starvation stared the Settlers in the face.

Whereas the might of the great British Empire had humbled the human inhabitants who dared to oppose it, the spirits of this African earth refused to nurture the foreign seeds forced down their throat!

The British authorities had to reconsider their strict conditions. The size of land grants increased, employment of the indigenous people was permitted and a more flexible attitude to moving away from the allocated land adopted. But the most significant change was from crop to animal farming, made possible by the increased land allocations. Once the cattle and sheep were brought in, the farmers prospered.

While many of the Settlers stayed in and around Algoa Bay (later called Port Elizabeth) some felt the need to venture further inland. After a long and arduous journey, a group dug their roots into the fertile highland under a spur of the great Drakensberg Mountain, named the "Elephant's Ear" because of its shape, in an area called East Griqualand.

The land was not lightly gained nor without controversy for the Griquas, a race of mixed European and Hottentot descent, had lived there as a semi-independent people, with the town of

Kokstad as their headquarters. But in 1878, giving in to pressure from other tribes and the white Settlers, the area was incorporated into the Province of the Cape of Good Hope and became part of the British colony in Southern Africa.

Among the first to plant their roots under the watchful eye in the Elephant's Ear was the Byron family. They named their farm "Byroncroft" and established what was to become a highly successful dairy farm.

A strange story known as the "Cattle Killing Delusion" is said to have depleted the might of the Xhosas who had once fought to keep the settlers out. One May-day in 1856 Nongquase, a young Xhosa woman, was gazing into the waters of the Gxara River, when she heard the whispering voices of the Ancestors coming from beneath the river stones. They foretold that the "white invaders" – and those who disobeyed orders from the "other world" – would be driven into the sea by a great wind. On a day still to be decided, Nongquase relayed to her Uncle Mhlakaze – the tribal witch doctor – a blood-red sun would rise, the fields would stand ready to reap, illness and old age would disappear. Dead chiefs would arise, kraals (enclosures) would be filled with cattle and pits overflow with grain. Mhlakaze, believing the prophesy, hurried to tell the Chief, who was also convinced that this was indeed a message from the Ancestors.

The Xhosas were overjoyed with the prospect of regaining their pride and their land. Many traveled to the Gxara River and they too told of seeing whole armies of warriors waiting to emerge from the water. Others said they saw horns of cattle mingling in the reeds. Some heard the bellowing and clashing of horns as the cattle waited in the secret caves beneath the riverbed. Those who lived near the sea, told of visions of returning heroes striding in the waves of the ocean.

But the sacrifice demanded of the Xhosa people, relayed by Nongquase, in preparation for this miracle needed an act of blind faith. Every head of livestock in the hands of the Xhosa nation was to be slain, and all grain and garden produce destroyed. Even the intervention of the British authorities and of the missionaries, learning of this proposed destruction, could not sway the belief in this prophesy. Perhaps it was the addition of the words "and those who disobeyed orders from the "other world", that led to such incomprehensible obedience. Special kraals were built to hold the cattle that would rise from the waters and huts were strengthened against the hurricane that was to come. An estimate puts the number of livestock slaughtered at over 200,000. The preparations done, time seemed to stand still as the whole Xhosa nation waited for the miracle.

The sun that rose on the day predicted by Nongquase (18 February 1857) was neither blood-red nor remarkable, there was no hurricane, nothing came out of the river or the sea, the dead chiefs still slept – and the white invaders remained.

he despair was all consuming! Massive starvation followed. Within six months, despite some relief efforts by the authorities, more than half the Xhosa population is said to have died. The military might of the Xhosa nation was broken, although some forays still occurred until the late 1870s. Many Xhosa went to work for the Settlers. They received in return shelter, basic rations and a monetary pittance.

A devastated and humbled Xhosa nation would have to wait 137 years for part of the prophesy to be fulfilled. Although he was not able to raise the dead chiefs, summon cattle from the water or fill the grain pits in one day, a great Xhosa man spearheaded the lifting of the yolk of the "white invaders" – not only from the necks of the Xhosa – but from the necks of all people of colour in the land. His name was Nelson Rolihlahla Mandela and it was a true miracle achieved with words, not weapons.

In 1994, the African National Congress, once a banned and denigrated organisation, with Mr Mandela as its leader, was voted into power in South Africa by an overwhelming majority. Surely the Ancestors celebrated with their descendants!

Chapter 2

In the early spring of 1910, the little town of Kokstad, East Griqualand waited for the life-giving rains. In the afternoons, clouds built behind the hills that encircled the town, and distant lightning strikes danced to the rumbling thunder, tantalising the rain-starved valley below. It had been a long and cold winter – heavy snow blanketing the hilltops and a mantle occasionally covering the valley. Although the warmer sun was welcome, only the rains would refresh and revive. For now, hope hovered on the horizon.

A ten-year-old boy shuffled home. Dust puffs swirled as he dejectedly kicks at the pebbles scattered along the dusty road leading to the cottage he now shared with his mother and two sisters. Standing at the door, Fanny was waiting impatiently for her son. At last, seeing him dawdling along she called: "Algie, hurry up, I have something to tell you."

Algie and Fanny embraced in the doorway, and clung to each other for a few moments. Both were trying to come to terms with the loss of a husband and father. How ironic mused Fanny, that her husband, George Arthur Peddie, a captain in the British Mounted Cavalry, having survived the perils of the Boer war, had succumbed to a bout of malaria. Now all the family have is a meagre pension and a tiny cottage in Kokstad.

Algie follows his mother into the dining room where his sisters, Evelyn and Doris, are already seated, eating the lunch prepared by their nanny, Themba. Algie, the middle child, starts to wolf down his lunch with all the relish of a constantly hungry growing lad.

"Uncle Raymond and I have been discussing what's best for both our families." Fanny's voice is sympathetic as she says this, but there is also an undercurrent of excitement, something that has been missing in their lives these past six months since their father's death. Fanny has just returned after spending a few weeks with her brother Raymond, the present owner of "Byroncroft", the farm that had been home to the Byron family since 1825. Fanny had helped with the funeral arrangements when Raymond's beloved wife, Kathleen, had died suddenly and cared for the bewildered four-year-old, Gerald, who wandered around searching for his mother.

Fanny's children, although glad to have their mother back home, were so used to being cared for by Themba that her absence had not been particularly disruptive. The only difference was that Themba brought her mattress and blankets from her small outside room and slept on the kitchen floor at night while their mother was away.

The children had loved their aunt. Christmas was always a time for the gathering of the family at

Byroncroft and they could not image Aunt Kathleen not being there.

"Uncle Raymond has asked us to go and live with him on the farm, so that I can look after Gerald for him." Fanny was unable to keep the joy out of her voice.

Algie was the first to register what was being said. He flung a half-eaten piece of bread back on the plate, sprung up and did a jig around the kitchen, shouting, "Hooray! Hooray!"

The girls' reaction was less spontaneous, especially 14-year-old Evelyn, always the practical one.

"Where would we go to school?" Eleven asked. Byroncroft lay some 50 miles from Kokstad, the nearest town of any consequence.

"We don't need to go to school," Algie replied quickly. "We could work on the farm."

"Oh yes, you do," laughed his mother. Turning to Evelyn she said, "Uncle Raymond suggested you might like to go as a boarder to St Mary's in Pietermaritzburg."

The reaction was what Fanny had expected. Evelyn was overjoyed. She had wanted to go to St Mary's but on a soldier's pension, Fanny had not been able to afford it. Pietermaritzburg was known for its exclusive boarding schools catering for the children of the elite civil servants, the well-heeled merchants and prosperous farmers.

"Algie and Doris, you will go to Miss Bream's farm school as weekly boarders." continued Fanny.

"Do I have to," pleaded Algie. "I could help Uncle Raymond much more if I stayed on the farm all the time."

"I could too," echoed Doris. She was quick to follow her brother's lead.

"You'll be home each weekend and for the holidays," replied their mother.

Both Algie and Doris had inherited a love of the land from their mother. They were never happier than when among the farm animals or helping tend the crops. Every year it was getting more difficult to drag the two of them away from the farm after their Christmas visits.

For Evelyn, the opportunity to join her friends at "St Mary's School for Young Ladies" was the fulfillment of her greatest desire.

"Are we all agreed then?" asked Fanny.

There were vigorous nods and happy smiles all round!

And so, the Peddie family – Fanny and her children Evelyn, Algie and Doris (and Themba), - moved to Byroncroft and joined Raymond Byron and his son Gerald on the farm whose pastures lay beneath the ever-imposing heights of the Elephant's Ear, one of the Drakensberg peaks. Themba was also very happy. She too was going home.

Chapter 3

As soon as he could escape from the "unpacking and settling in" that Fanny and Themba insisted he take part in, Algie headed for the stables. Although he loved all animals, he had a passion for horses.

Down the three steps from the veranda that fronted the north side of the six-bedroom farm house, with walls of local stone and an iron roof, through an area of lawn, beyond which lay a small garden, its flowers kept blooming with much hardship. Only the "used" – (mainly bath) water was permitted to nurture the plants, for the most pressing problem on the farm was the provision of sufficient water for man, beast and crops. Then on, past the many structures that had been added over the years – a variety of storage rooms for grain and equipment, the "dairy" where the household butter was made (and later also housed the generator when electric lights were installed), and a guest rondavel (a round structure with brown/red clay walls, smooth polished dung floors and a conical shaped thatched roof). These later buildings, more simply constructed than the farmhouse – but just as effective – had been built by the Xhosa servants, descendants of the once proud warrior Xhosa race now reconciled to being farm workers.

Algie opened the gate in the fence that surrounded the farmhouse and ran to the corrugated overhang that provided some shelter for the plough, tractor and other farm implements. He couldn't resist a very quiet tap on the triangular "wake-up gong". The daybreak crowing of the beady-eyed rooster, who lorded it over his harem of hens, came too late for the farm workers. They were awoken around 5am each morning by the sound of the gong – metal hitting metal – the important task given to one of the wives of Vuyo, the farm "headman". She was the keeper of the alarm clock!

Algie crossed a large square of earth with only patches of grass struggling to survive in the rain-starved land. On one side were the stables, as well as a stall for the bull and spare shelters~ used sometimes for sick cows. Kyas, the traditional Xhosa round houses with conical shaped thatched roofs, in which the farm workers and their extended families lived, lined the side furthest from the farmhouse. These structures were of brown/red clay, dung floors and straw roofs. Beyond this were the kraals (enclosures) where the herd of mainly Jersey cows was brought twice a day for milking. Attached to the kraals was the shed in which the milking was done.

Inside the stables Algie briefly greeted the two farm horses and the polo ponies, but he was headed for Dancer's stall. This was his uncle's prize polo pony. He stroked the proud, strong neck, and nestled his cheek against the sinuous shoulder. Dancer, so called because he could "turn on a tuppence" – a very important asset when on a polo field – made short friendly whinnying sounds and gently nuzzled Algie's back. They were soulmates.

With the purchase of a long coveted adjoining farm, Byroncroft now encompassed close to 2,000 hectares. The farmhouse stood on a small rise. The Elephants Ear dominated the distant horizon. When the sun cast a certain shadow on the spur, a dark blot was visible which looked like an eye between the "trunk" and the "ear" giving even more credence to the elephant-like description.

Algie was overjoyed to be on the farm. Whenever possible he was at Uncle Raymond's side, even at the early morning milking in the middle of winter when often a sprinkling of snow lay on the path. Uncle Raymond and Algie would don their heavy coats, hats, gloves and gum boots and, accompanied by the excited barking of the two Rhodesian Ridgeback dogs, crunch their way to the milking shed. There the cows and the herders would be waiting. Clothed in the blankets which had replaced the traditional animal skins, bare footed and often bare headed, the herders were usually standing shivering around a small fire they had built once the cows were in place.

The cows were all hand-milked by the skillful herders and the milk poured from the buckets into large containers. Every day, except Sunday, these were loaded onto a horse drawn cart and taken to the main road, some two miles away. The chugging of the large truck from the milk factory was a welcome sound to the already weary labourers. Most of the rich, creamy milk from Byroncroft was turned into cheese and butter. A smaller container was kept back to satisfy the needs of the household.

In the dry winter season, once the milk had been delivered and the all-important "imali nto" (receipt) brought back to Nkosi (Master), the cart was sent to the small stream which trickled its lazy way through a dip in the land. Large drums were filled with water and brought back for the use of the household, and to fill the animal troughs. It was back-breaking work. During the all too brief periods of rainfall, the precious liquid was collected in the storage tanks strategically placed around the farm, making life – temporarily – a lot easier for the labourers.

Now back on the farm where she was born and raised, Fanny saved from a miserable existence as a widow allocated a small pension and a tiny cottage in lieu of her husband's life given for his country, even if not in battle! She was home, no longer as the daughter of the house, but the "Nkosikazi", the term of respect used by the servants for the Madam of the house.

Fanny was again able to serve the generous "farm cooked" meals which hadn't been affordable on her widow's pension. While she did most of the cooking herself, there were five servants to help her run the house – the kitchen girl, the bedroom girl, the "rest of the house" girl, the "dairy" girl (who made the household's butter and cheese) and the garden girl ~ All family of the Xhosa men who toiled in the service of the Nkosi of Byroncroft. These were sought- after jobs, for which they received food and a pittance for their labours. And, of course, Themba helped with Gerald. Regardless of their ages the female servants were referred to as "girls" and the males "boys". Only the supervisor of the labourers, Vuyo, was called "The Headman".

For Themba, it was also a joyful homecoming. Her father had been one of the herders on the farm and her mother was Fanny's nursemaid. Themba and Fanny, being about the same age (no records were kept of the Xhosa births) had grown up almost as sisters. It was accepted that children of the farmers had close Xhosa friends of a similar age while growing up on the isolated farms. The language spoken was mostly the native one, learned at an early age from the nannies into whose care the children were placed. Being chosen as a companion to the children of the Nkosi was considered a great honour.

As adults, the roles reverted back to master/mistress and servant without any visible signs of conflict, but the bonds once forged often remained close. And so it was with Fanny and

Themba. When Fanny had left to complete her schooling, Themba helped with other tasks around the farm. A few years later she was given in marriage to a man from a nearby farm, once he had paid the "lobola" of several cattle to her father. She had four children in quick succession. Fanny married her cavalry officer and when she was expecting her first child, she sent for Themba. By this time, Themba's husband had taken a second wife, as was the Xhosa custom, so he had someone to look after him. Leaving her own children with their grandmother, Themba had gone to Kokstad, without hesitation, to look after Fanny's children. But now she was back on the farm and could see her own children every day. A new kya was built for Themba and her family. From being the lowly daughter of a herder she now, as the favourite servant of the Nkosikazi, had a position of power and prestige!

Gerald was a sickly child and demanded constant attention from both Fanny and Themba, which they gave willingly. When Fanny's own children protested that they felt neglected, they were scolded and told not to be selfish.

"How can you not feel sorry for a poor motherless boy." Fanny was shocked, "Don't you realise how much we have to thank Uncle Raymond for? All he asks in return is that I look after Gerald, and this I will do to the best of my ability.

Fanny had become so wrapped up in this task that she overlooked the fact that her own children had recently lost their beloved father. Fortunately, to a certain extent, Uncle Raymond became a substitute father figure, especially to Algie. Only Themba seemed to understand their need, but she had her hands full with the petulant Gerald. All three, particularly Doris, often sought the comfort of their beloved nanny.

Algie spent as much times as could with his uncle's horses. Uncle Raymond often took Algie with him when he rode to the furthest corners of his large farm, checking that all was in order. Algie was a fearless rider – sometimes too overconfident – but he had a way with horses. Being a cavalryman, his father had taught all his children to ride from a young age, although they were not able to keep horses of their own. And of course, they all went to the polo matches that were a regular diversion of the "gentlemen farmers".

CHAPTER 4

For the first few years, life on the farm was idyllic for Algie. Uncle Raymond took him under this wing and taught him how to run the farm. Even at aged ten he was tall and strong. Over the years as he helped lift bales of hay, fill the water tanks from the stream, guide the heavy plough, join the herders in forcing the bull back into the stall after the mating season and doing a multitude of other tasks, he developed into an extremely fit and muscular young man. Uncle Raymond also taught Algie how to handle the guns kept on the farm. His favourite was the rifle used to supplement the meat pot with guinea fowl and dove. The large shotgun was sometimes needed to end the suffering of an injured or sick animal. The handgun – which it was hoped would never be needed – was for protection from intruders. The guns had been in the Byron family for many years and Algie took over the necessary task of keeping them clean and polished. With his good eyes, Algie could "bag" a guinea fowl on demand and dove pie was often on the menu!

There was time to play as well. His Xhosa friend was Sphiwe, eldest son of the headman, Vuyo. It was a dangerous alliance for both were totally fearless, stubborn and too adventurous. Mostly they played some sort of ball game, with Algie often having trouble outplaying the skillful twisting and turning of the nimble Sphiwe – much to his disgust!

One of their favourite pastimes was making models of fighting bulls from the rich river clay. These had to nestle comfortably into the palm of their hands. They would search for bones, stones or any sharp objects from which to fashion the horns and hooves. Sphiwe's bull would be faithfully formed, the clay smoothed and the horns and hooves in their correct places. Algie's bull was lumps of clay of different sizes slapped together – he had no artistic talents, nor the patience to "fiddle around" as he called it. Once the clay had hardened in the sun, they would match their bulls against each other. No quarter was given on either side and, needless to say, their hands suffered from many cuts and bruises caused by blows from the sharp horns and hooves – until at last one of the bulls shattered. Often the bulls were discarded and the dispute resolved in "physical combat". Whereas Algie may have been bigger and stronger, Sphiwe was more agile and cunning. But there was honour among combatants, neither would admit as to how their wounds and bruises were caused.

One day, the two boys were sitting on an outcrop of rocks, from where the best view of the Elephant's Ear could be seen. It was a sunny afternoon and the "eye" was dark and forbidding.

Behind them was a small rockface, protected by a natural overhang. On the walls of this rockface were paintings of stick-like figures, a legacy left by the nomadic Bushmen who are generally regarded as the original inhabitants of most of Southern Africa. The Bushmen ~ small of statue (rarely over 5 feet), wrinkled in appearance, having extraordinarily keen eyesight, skill as trackers and a sense of music ~ painted their stories in caves or on protected rockfaces. The excellence of the drawings is exceptional given they were created by a seemingly primitive, nomadic race. The painting on this particular rockface was a hunting scene ~ the black stick figures throwing their spears at the prey, then carrying the buck – legs bound and hanging upside down – on a branch borne by two men. One unexplained figure, painted white, seemed to be a man with an animal head and was shown in an almost frenzied pose. Bushmen paintings, when in good condition, are very valuable, but the overhang on this rockface was crumbling away and the resulting exposure to the elements had left the mural chipped and stained.

The attention of Algie and Sphiwe was, however, focused on the Elephant's Ear. "The mountain often calls to me," said Sphiwe.

"Mountains can't call to you," scoffed Algie. Then added, "I wonder what the "eye" really is? There must be some reason why it is so black at times."

"It is the cave of a very terrible witchdoctor," Sphiwe answered.

"He has the body of a man, but can change himself into an animal" for such was the belief of the Xhosas in the area.

An idea prickled Algie's imagination. "Let's go and see if it's true."

Sphiwe was visibly shaken. "Too far," he muttered. It was a long way to the foothills and the climb up the face of the cliff to the "eye" looked very steep.

"You are afraid to go," taunted Algie. "Do you think the Spirit of the Mountain will eat you?"

"Come, I will show you the Spirit." Sphiwe led Algie to the rockface and pointed to the white stick figure of the man with the animal head.

"There he is. How do you think someone can put him on a rock if he is not real?" he asked triumphantly.

Algie looked long and hard at the strange stick figure. He had been around the Xhosa people long enough to respect their intuition and beliefs. But his curiosity got the better of him.

"I am going to find out if it's true. You can go and hide behind your mother's skirt if you are afraid."

The reaction was what Algie had hoped for.

"I'm not afraid!" stormed Sphiwe "We will go and look into the Elephant's eye, but..."

"But what?"

"We must make good plans first."

Algie and Sphiwe argued long and hard about the best way to tackle the mission. Algie knew that Uncle Raymond would not give him permission to climb the steep and dangerous rock-covered slopes of the Elephant's Ear, so he would have to find some excuse to be away overnight. He and Sphiwe were in agreement that it was a two-day trip there and back.

Algie was already having second thoughts as he stared at the forbidding heights that led to the "eye". But there was no turning back now. Neither of the boys could accept being called a coward. They were so engrossed in their planning that they didn't realise the sun had almost set and they had missed the milking. They flew on swift feet to receive their just desserts – Algie a tongue lashing from Uncle Raymond and Sphiwe firm blows from his father, Vuyo.

But they were firm in their resolve to one day explore the "Eye of the Elephant".

Chapter 5

Many of those who made up the East Griqualand farming community attended the local church on the scheduled occasions when a minister visited the hinterland communities. It was an opportunity to mix and mingle with people they rarely saw. Many were related in this close-knit community.

However, it was the sports days and the special celebrations that were the highlights of their otherwise secluded life.

It was also a time for young people to meet, form an affinity and hopefully marry.

Lawn tennis had been introduced to South Africa in the 1880s, with clubs springing up in the Cape, then in Natal and the Transvaal. As early as 1881 the first South African championships took place. But it was the tour to South Africa by an English tennis team in 1908, and a South African finalist in the men's singles at the 1912 Olympic Games in Stockholm – with C.L. Winslow eventually the winner ~ that induced tennis fever in the East Griqualand farming community. A piece of land next door to the polo club was procured and the community bonded together to lay down four tennis courts. And so, Lawn tennis was added to the polo playing past-times of the farming gentry. Even though the surface of the courts was clay, not lawn, nevertheless it remained "Lawn tennis".

The get-togethers, held usually monthly on a Sunday, were a time for excesses, particularly the midday meal, with the ladies vying with each other to produce the most succulent vittles. Morning and afternoon teas ran a close second in variety and competitiveness.

In contrast to the polo playing fraternity whose focus was on procuring the best polo ponies, tennis added a new dimension in competitiveness ~ and its focus wasn't so much on the game itself, but on the accoutrements. Even as a rural tennis club, compliance to the laid down rules and conventions of Lawn tennis was expected. Tennis dresses, at first, were required to be ankle length. A photo of Fanny, dressed in a high necked, long sleeved and ankle-length tennis dress, complemented by a wide brimmed sun hat, hung in her bedroom. Nevertheless, the length of the dress had to be well below the knee and of course, only white attire was allowed for both men and women. White shirts, long white trousers and white socks for the men, and all wore the regulation rubber soled tennis shoes. The racquets were wood framed and strung with gut.

Whereas most of the younger generation had learned to play tennis as part of their schooling, many of the not-so-young had missed out. One of the courts was set aside at certain times as a "teaching court" with an innovative young man offering his services as a "tutor".

Special occasions such as a wedding, a memorable anniversary or a funeral were also a reason to "down tools". The close knit and inter-related farming community made the most of these occasions to leave the demanding duties of the farm behind and escape for a day or two. With the long distances that separated the farms, an overnight stay was sometimes necessary.

Sale days added another dimension, for not only the gentlemen farmers would attend, but all the diverse and often overlooked "others" who made up the East Griqualand farming community. On these days, there was comradeship and mingling, views and advice exchanged, bargains sought and bought. But it was also often a sad day, for a sale was usually the result of misfortune – perhaps a death with no one to carry on the duties on the farm or ~ worse still ~ bankruptcy. Nevertheless, it was a time for some badly needed social intermingling. Sale days were also a chance to restock and thus retain some of the animals and implements in the community.

The opportunity for the boys to explore the "eye" came when the family was invited to spend a weekend with relations who were celebrating a 25th wedding anniversary. Uncle Raymond was at last persuaded to attend when Algie offered to stay behind to help Vuyo. Algie realised that this was the ideal opportunity to discover the secret of the

Elephant's Eye. But they still had to hatch a plan to persuade Vuyo to let them go.

As soon as the family left on Saturday morning, Sphiwe and Algie started on their chores as usual. Then Sphiwe, after returning the herd of cows to the fields, reported to his father that he had seen what looked like smoke coming from the boundary of the farm nearest to the Elephants Ear. Algie pretended to be very worried, and insisted that he and Sphiwe go and investigate. Veld fires were always a danger and Vuyo was unable to resist the forcefulness of Algie's argument, so hesitatingly agreed. Algie instructed the maids to fill two rucksacks with supplies. Tying a blanket each behind the saddles, with Algie slinging his hunting rifle around his body, the boys mounted the farm horses and headed in the direction of the "fire". As soon as they were out of sight of the farmhouse, they doubled back to the rural roads that circumnavigated the farms. This was the longer way to the mountain, but they had no option. The barbed wire boundary of Byroncroft could not be crossed on horseback. Their destination lay beyond the farm's boundaries ~ in the no-man's land of the Elephant's Ear.

It was a late autumn day. The early morning chill gradually gave way to the lazy sun as its rays brushed away the light morning mist. At first the pair rode excitedly, racing each other over the flat stretches, but once they left the road and headed towards the hills, the path grew stony and they were forced to carefully negotiate the rougher bits. The sun had passed its zenith when they eventually reached the foothills. Both boys were awed by the elevation that grew taller and more challenging as they approached it. And the dark menacing "eye" seemed to follow their every move. Algie found himself waiting for the "elephant" to flap its ears, like those in the wild did when they sensed intruders!

They crossed a small stream and while the horses drank their fill, the boys satisfied their hunger from the bounty in their bags. Soon the climb grew too steep and narrow for the horses. Tethering them in the shade of a large tree, the boys left them contentedly grazing on the still-green grass.

It was Sphiwe who made the first move. "Come, the sun is growing old. We still have far to go."

Taking the rifle, the rucksacks and the blankets with them they started their climb. At first it was relatively easy, for both boys were fit and strong. But soon the grass cover gave way to rocky outcrops, which in turn gave way to large boulders. The boys climbed steadily and carefully. They were so engrossed in trying to negotiate the narrow passes and avoid falling off the ledges, they didn't have the time or energy to think about what might lurk in the "eye".

At last they stood just below where the eye should be. Their view was obscured by an overhang that stood between them and the summit of the mountain. Although they tried several alternative routes, to their immense disappointment, there didn't seem to be a way to reach the "eye".

"We should have brought rimpies," said Algie. These were strong ropes made from the treated and dried hide of cattle.

"What could you do with a rimpie?" asked Sphiwe.

"We could throw it around that branch jutting out of the rock and climb up the rope." Algie had seen pictures of intrepid rock climbers.

Sphiwe almost fainted at the thought!

Then they heard it. A faint chanting, coming from above them. Both Algie and Sphiwe froze in fear. The chanting grew louder and it seemed to come from inside the mountain. The boys crept to an overhang of rock with some bushes close by and clung together in abject terror.

It was unclear who got the bigger fright ~ the apparition who "parted the bushes" revealing a path through a cleft in the rock ~ or the two boys clinging to each other under the overhang.

Only later Algie remembered the words the "thing" spoke. The first were in Xhosa: "You come a day early" and then "Good God! Who are you?" in English! This was immediately followed by wild gesticulations of the wildebeest tail switch he carried, together with menacing prancing and the chanting of illegible words.

Sphiwe hid his face, too frightened to look upon the apparition, but Algie's curiosity got the better of him. He slowly opened one eye and by turning his head slightly could see where the noise was coming from.

The apparition did look something like the drawing of the half man, half animal on the rockface. He wore the white clothes of a witchdoctor, but unlike any witchdoctor Algie had ever seen, seemed to have an animal mask draped over his head. Algie couldn't decide what animal it looked like – something between a hyena and an eagle was his best guess.

The dancing and chanting grew slower and slower as the witchdoctor seemed to run out of breath. He started to cough uncontrollably, until eventually he almost fell to the ground. Algie disentwined himself from Sphiwe's grip and, impulsively, went to help the "man/animal" in trouble. After a few feeble attempts to fend Algie off, the old man – that much was evident to Algie – accepted help in being led to sit in the shade of the overhang. Algie reclined in front of him, being careful to keep his head below that of the witchdoctor's – an indication of respect.

After a while, when his breathing was more normal, the witchdoctor asked: "Who are you?" in Xhosa.

Sphiwe, who had been terrified as he watched Algie's interaction with the apparition, now slowly crawled to lie next to Algie as he heard the non-threatening tone of the question.

"Nkosi," Sphiwe replied with courtesy and humility, "I am eSphiwe, and my brother is eAlgie. Our home is the farm of many cows that lies in the shelter of the Elephant's Ear."

"Do you not know this place is sacred?"

Sphiwe hesitated, trying to find a way to make their mission acceptable.

"The mountain elephant often calls to me," he said, remembering what had started them on this forbidden journey.

And Algie added, "We wanted to look into its eye".

There was a long silence. So long that Sphiwe was sure the witchdoctor was preparing a terrible spell to place upon them.

Suddenly high pitched, whistling sounds seemed to come from all around them.

"What's happening?" Algie asked, sensing that Sphiwe was not too concerned.

"The witchdoctor has sent the Nomototlo to gather the knowledge he wants." Sphiwe replied. "They are bringing back the messages."

Algie had heard vague rumours about the Nomototlo, the messengers of the witchdoctors. He tried to remember what he knew about them. Spirits no bigger than walnuts... Sent around the world to gather knowledge... Respond in high pitched whistling sounds... A suspicion that the witchdoctor, to produce the frightening sounds they were now hearing, used ventriloquism.

The whistling sounds stopped suddenly, but the ringing in the boys' ears continued for some time.

"You tell the truth," pronounced the witchdoctor. Then announced, "My name is Lo Lindi, and my home is the sacred Mountain of the Elephant."

He seemed to go into a trance. After a while he opened his eyes and, pointing to Algie with his switch said, "You are the child of the daughter of Thenjwa".

Algie was astounded. Thenjwa – meaning one who can be trusted – was the name given to his late grandfather by the Xhosas.

"Did you know my grandfather?" Algie plucked up the courage to ask.

There was no answer to Algie's question. All that was said was:

"Those who come to this sacred place must bring gifts."

Algie's mind's eye went through his pockets, but all he had was his trusty old pocket knife, some matches and a dirty handkerchief. He didn't think Sphiwe had anything on him worthy to be called a gift. He was conscious of the rifle still slung across his back, but that wasn't his to give – even to curry the favour of a witchdoctor.

Then he had a bright idea. It would be worth a try.

"We have food," he said. He carefully laid the rifle on the ground, pulled the rucksack from his back and placed it before Lo Lindi. Sphiwe quickly followed suit.

"Show me!" commanded Lo Lindi.

Both boys proceeded to unlatch the rucksacks and laid the contents before the witchdoctor.

Algie was not sure that the supplies they had would appease a witchdoctor. Weren't they supposed to live on strange things like animal hearts and tongues ~ or insects – and to drink blood? He had never really had much to do with these "spiritual people".

Algie viewed the "gifts" in some dismay. While there was mielie (maize) bread and some biltong (dried and salted beef), the bulk was made up of fancy iced cakes, spice biscuits, fruit cake and other "treats" that his mother had left him.

He was very surprised when Lo Lindi almost reverently picked up one of the iced cakes, licked off the icing and slowly consumed the soft delicacy. That jolted Algie's memory and he recalled the English words the witchdoctor had spoken when he had first seen them.

"It is very good," pronounced Lo Lindi.

That gave Algie the courage to ask, "May we go to see the eye of the elephant?" For he was sure the way to the cave was through the bushes that had been "parted" by the witchdoctor.

"That is not permitted," was the reply. "Only those who are pursued unjustly and fear for their life, but know their heart is pure, may take refuge in the eye."

Both boys were bitterly disappointed. Neither felt they fitted the criteria for entry!

"Nkosi," Sphiwe asked, "The eye of the elephant is always watching over us, but sometimes it grows dark and threatening. What is the meaning of the darkness in its eye?"

"The wonderful and the impossible have come into collision," answered Lo Lindi, then appeared to slip into a trance again.

"What does he mean?", Algie asked Sphiwe.

"I have asked a question that is very difficult to answer," was the reply.

Suddenly Lo Lindi stood up and ordered the boys to gather firewood. They hastened to obey.

Algie was the first to return. He couldn't contain his curiosity any longer, so he asked, in English, "Sir, did you know my grandfather?"

"He was a good man," came the reply, in perfect English.

Suddenly realising what he had said, Lo Lindi turned on Algie and, reverting to Xhosa, he spat our angrily, "You tricked me!" and then calming a little asked, "How did you know?"

Algie repeated the words that he had first heard Lo Lindi speak.

Just then Sphiwe returned with a large bundle of firewood.

Immediately, the old man took on the mantle of the "witchdoctor" again. With much ritual and chanting, he built a fire and lit it seemingly by catching a ray of the fast-disappearing sun and throwing it on the grass and wood.

Algie was impressed. Whoever had taught this white man the skills of a witchdoctor had done an excellent job.

"I will accept your gifts of food," said Lo Lindi, "but they are not fit to fill the stomach of a growing man-child. Tonight, we will eat my food."

Lo Lindi plucked three thin, still green branches from a tree. He used these to skewer three pieces of some sort of meat, which he roasted over the fire.

"I wonder what meat it is?", whispered Algie to Sphiwe.

Do not wonder," Sphiwe advised. "Just eat." To him they looked like giant rats!

The meat was surprising good. Both boys were very hungry after their exhausting climb. Lo Lindi also shared the mielie bread and biltong, but the delicacies he kept for himself. Algie realised that it was most probably many years since the old man had tasted such fare.

Lo Lindi showed them where a small stream trickled out from a fissure in the rockface, and they drank deeply of the clear, sweet tasting spring water.

The three sat contentedly around the fire for a while, then Lo Lindi said, "I will return to my cave, for the night grows cold. You will sleep here, but do not leave the mountain or try to follow me. Tomorrow I will come and answer your question." And disappeared into the bushes.

Sphiwe was the first to voice his concern, "Do you think the witchdoctor will turn into his animal half and come to harm us in the night?"

Algie could reply with confidence, "No, the witchdoctor is a good man."

Sphiwe was in agreement, "Yes, I feel that too."

Algie's thought was along different lines. "Shall we creep through the bushes to the hole in the mountain? It will lead us to the eye."

"NO!" The reply was so abrupt and dismissive that Algie felt he had to argue his case.

"But we've come so far and we know that the eye is a cave where Lo Lindi lives. It's so near. How can we not go all the way?"

Sphiwe was silent for a long time, then he said, "I cannot explain it. You will not understand when I say the mountain is trying to tell me something. All I know is that I must respect the witchdoctor and his sacred place."

That was enough reason to quell any further arguments from Algie.

The boys rolled themselves up in their blankets. As the light of the fire ebbed away, the full moon rose, bathing the landscape in silver and gray.

As he hovered on the edge of sleep, Algie tried to piece together the puzzle that was Lo Lindi. Even his name was strange. Trying to translate it from Xhosa into English it sounded like "That Lindi". As he slowly repeated the name, suddenly an idea came to him. Lo ... Lord...Lindi. Was he perhaps an English nobleman who had been sent to Africa on some errand and somehow been accepted into a Xhosa tribe? Or perhaps he was a – what had his mother called it – a remittance man? Someone who had disgraced his family in England and was sent to Africa to "disappear'. Mother had said the name came from the regular "remittances" of money they received in exchange for never returning home. Who had taught Lo Lindi the skills of a witchdoctor and why should he live in that cave?

Other thoughts swirled. Why hadn't Lo Lindi heard or seen them as they climbed up the hill? Or sensed them with his witching powers? Then a possible explanation came. Was he expecting someone to bring him supplies? He remembered the first words were about being a day early. The puzzle was too difficult for Algie's exhausted mind.

Eventually the boys slept, awakened now and then by the hoot of the owls as they used the darkness to swoop down on their prey, or the other sound that came from the cave above – chanting that went on intermittently throughout the night.

Chapter 6

"Makulu, uphi isidudu, makulu, uphi isidudu"

The cooing of the Cape Turtle doves awoke the boys, just as the sun began to tear away the cobweb of mist that hid the valley below.

"I wish we did have some porridge" said Algie. For the meaning of the words the Xhosas gave to the cooing of the doves was "Grandmother, where's the porridge?"

"Uhambo lude", agreed Sphiwe, "The journey is long. And we have no food."

They drank from the stream, splashed a little of the ice-cold water over their faces and sat down to wait for the witchdoctor, using their blankets to shield them from the still cold air.

The boys didn't see the bushes part, but suddenly Lo Lindi was there. Algie was disappointed that he still wore his animal head. He had hoped to see the face of the old man.

Lo Lindi brought with him a large clay pot filled with phutu ~ porridge made from ground corn and cooked until it has a crumbly appearance. He placed it before the boys and from a dried pumpkin gourd he poured amasi – milk left in the sun for several days until curdled – over the phutu.

"Today, our phutu will taste as if we have a gift from the honey bee," announced Lo Lindi, and mixed a little honey taken from Algie's bag into the clay pot.

The boys waited for Lo Lindi to eat his share, using his hand as a ladle. Then it was their turn, and the scoops of porridge made hasty trips from their hands to their mouths, stilling the hunger pangs.

"We thank you for sharing your food with us, Nkosi," said Sphiwe humbly.

"Yes," Algie hastened to add, "I, too, offer you thanks."

Lo Lindi nodded almost imperceptibly. He seemed reserved and troubled.

Taking a long traditional Xhosa pipe from the pocket of his robe, Lo Lindi slowly filled it with some leaves. He seemed to blow into the pipe and suddenly it ignited. He slowly inhaled a few times. The boys waited anxiously.

At last Lo Lindi spoke.

"Last night, Sphiwe, you asked me a question that has troubled me. I have called on the Ancestors for their advice, and this is what I must say to you."

Lo Lindi eyes took on a faraway look and his words an ancient, husky, trembling timbre:

"Dark clouds are dancing on the horizon, white danger is hovering, you will need swift feet. The eye of darkness will be your ray of hope".

Sphiwe was trembling with fear, "I do not understand, Nkosi. What does it mean?"

But the "witchdoctor" had returned. He appeared to grow angry, and with much gesticulating, chanting and prancing, shouted, "Leave my mountain now!"

Grabbing their blankets, the now empty rucksacks and the rifle, the boys hastened to obey. At first, the way down was even more difficult than the ascent, with both boys slipping and sliding over the treacherous rocks, but eventually they reached the horses. Out of breath and overawed by the whole experience, they rested for a while in silence.

Eventually Sphiwe asked fearfully, "What did the words mean?"

Algie couldn't remember exactly what had been said, but certain words jumped out at him – dark clouds; danger – white danger – what was that? – ray of hope. The last sentence he remembered well.

"Do not worry, Sphiwe," said the ever confident Algie, "Remember whatever happens, Lo Lindi said "the eye of darkness will be your ray of hope."

"But what does it mean?" Sphiwe was not so easily placated.

"It must have something to do with the cave," guessed Algie.

Then, to avoid more difficult questions, Algie jumped to his feet saying, "It also means if we don't start immediately on our way back to the farm, we will face both black and white danger – from Vuyo and my uncle, if he is back before us."

Little did he know that he had defined the source of the white danger.

The ride back was subdued, but as they came in sight of the farmhouse, they conjured up what they hoped was a plausible story. Vuyo was so relieved to see them home safe and sound that he didn't ask too many questions. Fortunately, the family had not yet returned.

Their adventure to the "eye of the elephant" remained a secret between Algie and Sphiwe. Vuyo conveniently forgot to mention the boys' absence. He knew he had been misled.

For Algie, who had been so overjoyed to come to the farm, there were many disappointments as the years went by. The greatest was that his mother became totally absorbed with Gerald. And Gerald grew up to be spoilt, spiteful and devious. From a very young age he looked for ways to drive a wedge between Algie and Fanny. He constantly taunted Algie, and even with the best will in the world, the quick tempered Algie often found himself retaliating. Then Gerald would run crying to Fanny. In Fanny's eyes Gerald could do no wrong, so harsh words would be spoken, with Fanny beginning to believe that her son – once so happy and loving ~ was turning into an unpleasant bully.

Once he reached high-school age, Algie was sent to complete his education in Pietermaritzburg, but not to the elite school that Gerald would later attend., Fanny and Uncle Raymond had decided that as he was an indifferent scholar, an appropriate school for Algie was the "College". Evelyn was mortified to have a brother at that school – she and her friends only associated with the boys of "The Saint's" – as the elite boy's school was known. Algie was constantly in trouble with the teaching staff as he looked for ways to alleviate the boredom he felt when confined within the school walls, listening to things he had no interest in. Fortunately, he was a natural sportsman. His good eye and nimble feet contributed to many victories for his school as he ran in tries, hit sixes or peppered the bulls eye at the rifle range. He was also a good tennis player, although that sport was looked down upon at the College.

Aggravating his discontent was the fact that he only got back to the farm in the all too short school holidays, for Pietermaritzburg was a considerable distance away from his beloved Byroncroft.

But the long Christmas holidays came around regularly. An added delight for Algie was the first week of the new year, when their second cousins, Maud and Angela, came to stay. For as long as he could remember Algie had loved Maud, who was a year older than him. And Maud enjoyed the "puppy dog" devotion of the tall, strong boy who looked much older than his years. Maud was full of fun, at times quite unconventional, and always concocting things to do around the farm. She was a tomboy who rode horses just as well as Algie, matched him shot for shot in their "dove pie" expeditions, and often "refereed" the bull fights between Sphiwe and Algie – while still retaining her femininity and grace.

Dressing for the evening meal had been a custom at Byroncroft for as long as anyone could remember and Fanny continued to follow the tradition. As sunset approached and the family laid down tools for the day, the maids would carry the baths and the warm water to the bedrooms of the women, while the men used the washroom. As if in response to a godmother's wand, the plain, often dirty working clothes would transform into jacket, ties and long trousers for the menfolk, while the ladies donned their evening frocks and jewelry. Fanny always wore the drop pendant diamond necklace and matching earrings her mother had given her on her wedding day – a family heirloom that Evelyn would one day inherit.

After dinner, all would sit around the piano, with Fanny starting the ball rolling by playing some classical music. Then the girls would take turns with more modern songs. Here Algie came into his own. Fanny had tried to teach him to play the piano in a formal way, but he had no patience with scales, or with trying to interpret black spots written on a piece of paper. But as soon as he heard a tune he could pick out the correct notes on the keyboard, so he always ended up being quite the centre of attention, which he loved!

While Maud was a joy to have around, Angela was withdrawn, subject to mood swings, and preferred to have her nose in a book. The strange thing was that she seldom seemed to get very far into the story. Sphiwe, particularly, seemed to fear her and would go out of his way to avoid her. Algie once asked Sphiwe about this. He was surprised when Sphiwe replied,

"She has the devil in her." Prophetic words.

Chapter 7

The year was 1914. The dark clouds of war were gathering over Europe – and the rumbling thunder of the war machines would reach even into the tranquility of rural communities like East Griqualand.

When King George V, as head of the British Empire, declared war on Germany in August 1914, South Africa was automatically expected to support the Empire. However, there was still considerable bitterness resulting from the wars between Boer and British, even though by 1910 an agreement had been reached and the Union of South Africa established as a member of the Empire. Spurred on by the visions of an alleged prophet, Niklaas van Rensburg – who foretold of the collapse of the British Empire – an insurrection (known as "The Rebellion") started to fester in elements of the South African population. This came to a head in September 1914 when the Prime Minister announced the intention of the Union to invade the German-held South West Africa. However, there was little co-ordination between the leaders of the rebellion, and the last "Rebels" surrendered in early 1915.

East Griqualand was home to many farmers of British ancestry and numerous fathers, sons and even some mothers and daughters responded to the bugle call. They joined the legions of whites, coloureds and a native labour contingent who enlisted to defend the Empire. Some replaced the local British Imperial Garrison, on duty in South Africa, who returned to their homeland to fight alongside their countrymen. Others helped suppress the Rebellion. Although an enemy territory directly adjoined the Union, it was not until January 1915 that a double attack was made – by land and sea – on German South West Africa. German East Africa, under the leadership of Colonel Paul Emil von Lettow-Vorbeck – whose achievements were in the guerilla type war he fought – was never defeated. He only surrendered on 13 November 1918 after hearing of the capitulation of Germany.

During the war years Pietermaritzburg, as a recruiting post, was abuzz with military activity – uniformed officers, soldiers in varied dress and volunteers hoping to be accepted. Regaled by stories from soldiers injured or returning on leave, Algie saw only the adventurous side and was determined to join the Forces. He would follow in his father's footsteps and become a "Cavalry Man". When told he would have to wait until he was 18 he was devastated.

Thus, a new game was played regularly at Byroncroft. Algie was a brave British soldier, astride his horse, vanquishing the cowardly German soldier (Sphiwe) who dared to oppose him. When Sphiwe asked if he could sometimes win, Algie always replied that if you were a German you had to lose.

Not everyone had Algie's confidence in those early years of the war!

Algie was 15 when he committed what to Evelyn was his greatest iniquity. It was towards the end of Evelyn's final year at school and the annual farewell ball was to be held in the local town hall. Regardless of the still raging war, a splendid affair was planned, with Fanny having to dip deeply into her precious savings to buy Evelyn an elaborate ball gown. It was a very important event in Evelyn's life. She was to be partnered by a highly eligible officer. Parents were invited as well, so Fanny and Raymond undertook a special trip to Pietermaritzburg. Maud was also attending the ball but Algie, being only a "College boy" and a bit young was not eligible as a partner.

Whether it was a desire to spite Evelyn or a need to impress Maud, the idea that had been rambling in Algie's head refused to go away. He was foolish enough to confide in some of his College mates, and immediately the idea was hailed as a "must do".

The ball was in full swing. The reflections of the ornately dressed maidens were captured by the crystals of the cascading chandelier and complimented by the backdrop of the tastefully decorated historic town hall. The handsome young men were formally dressed, many in the uniform of the local Cavalry unit. An orchestra played polkas, waltzes and, occasionally, a more daring modern tune. Parents were seated around the walls.

Fanny, watching her daughter dancing in the arms of the officer, felt tears welling in her eyes as she remembered how she and her husband had danced in similar circumstances. Raymond's memories of his beloved wife were also rekindled. But despite sad memories, both were proud to be sharing this milestone in Evelyn's life.

Suddenly there was a commotion on the steps outside. Then a sharp "clip, clop" reverberated through the hall. The musicians, who were facing the entrance, stopped playing in amazement as two apparitions appeared – horsemen draped in white sheets with holes cut out where eyes should be. As the horses trotted onto the dance floor, with the "ghosts" uttering the most bloodcurdling sounds, dancers scattered in alarm – the gentlemen hurrying their partners to safety.

Evelyn's officer was the first to react by retrieving a ceremonial sword from a table. He challenged the horsemen and ordered them to leave. Other officers followed his lead. The horsemen decided that discretion outweighed valour and they spurred their steeds for a quick escape.

Two unfortunate things happened during the "retreat". The sheet covering one of the riders was whipped off by a sword-wielding officer – revealing a laughing Algie – and the second was that one of the horses left a messy trademark behind!

But a quick clean-, the comforting of the frightened maidens and the stifling of the amusement of those who saw the funny side, soon had things on track again. It remained one of St Mary's most memorable farewell balls.

It took Evelyn several years to forgive Algie for the embarrassment he caused. It also drove another wedge between Fanny and Algie. Not only was he a spiteful bully but he had ruined his sister's ball. Of the people close to Algie only Maud, Uncle Raymond and Evelyn's officer admitted to seeing the funny side.

The Christmas holidays that followed the disrupted ball was an unhappy time for Algie as he became more estranged from his mother. But as 1916 came rolling in, he started to look forward to Maud's visit, even if he had to put up with Angela who was becoming weirder each year. He had no premonition that this was to be a life-changing year.

The visitors had only been there a few days, when Algie realised that Sphiwe was obviously upset about something. He eventually confided in Algie that Angela was following him around. Algie told him not to be stupid. Why would a white girl follow a black boy around? Neither had an answer to this.

It was a particularly languid Sunday afternoon. The extended family had enjoyed an exceptionally good meal prepared by Fanny and the kitchen maids. On a Sunday, the main meal was always served at midday. This gave the kitchen maids their one afternoon off, once the dishes had been washed and stored away.

Algie, Evelyn, Doris, Maud, Angela and Gerald were sitting under the sheltering arms of the enormous fir tree in the farmhouse garden. It provided some relief from the relentless summer sun, which was only starting its slide toward the cool of the evening.

"Let's go for a swim in the river," suggested Maud. "Is the water hole deep enough?" (This only happened after good summer rains.)

"Great idea! Yes, it is." replied Algie, and got up immediately to make the necessary arrangements – for the only part of their stream deep enough to provide a "swimming hole" was quite a long way from the farmhouse.

"Where's Sphiwe?" asked Angela.

The unexpected question stopped Algie in his tracks. Faint alarm bells rang in this mind, but he dismissed them immediately. His thoughts were firmly fixed on the vision of Maud in her bathing suit. She had the loveliest long shapely legs and ... well, better not to think about the rest!

"I don't know," he replied. Then as an afterthought, "He usually spends his Sunday afternoons in the shed behind the stables, making those strange clay toys he tries to sell when we go to Matatiele." This was the closest town where, usually twice a month Uncle Raymond did his local shopping. Algie and Sphiwe were often taken along to load the heavy supplies.

Algie was to regret ever offering this piece of information.

In fact, the toys Sphiwe made were excellent replicas of animals, people or anything else that took his fancy, for he was very artistic. However, business was not good. Only the few tourists who braved the rough roads through Matatiele showed any interest in exchanging a few coins for the models.

"Anyway, let's get ready to go to the river. I'll hitch Old Joe to the cart." Algie hurried away.

"And I'll pack us a picnic tea," Doris set off for the kitchen.

When they were all excitedly piling into the cart, Algie noticed that Angela was not there.

"Where's Angela?" he called impatiently.

"She's not coming – says she has a headache." Doris offered this explanation.

Algie was secretly relieved. It would make the picnic even more enjoyable. As he spurred Old Joe on, he couldn't suppress the feeling of excitement. But once again he felt that something was not quite right. However, those thoughts were overridden by the pleasure of the moment. Maud sitting close to him in the driving seat, the rest of the party singing happy songs in the back, the sun shining, a delicious afternoon tea to look forward to ... life seemed perfect.

They had to come back earlier than planned. Gerald was feeling neglected and had spoilt the outing by complaining, shortly after afternoon tea, that he had a tummy ache. This had always brought him attention. Maud persuaded him to lie down in the shade, but when – to his amazement – everyone left him alone and continued to enjoy themselves. He threw a tantrum. This was such a regular occurrence that no one took any notice. He then threatened that if they didn't take him home immediately, he would tell Aunt Fanny that they had been cruel to him. Still no one took any notice. It was only when he started to sob inconsolably that Evelyn couldn't stand it any longer. She took pity on him and – as the eldest and technically in charge – decided that they should go back to the farmhouse.

A much more subdued group returned. Gerald had won again!

Algie met Uncle Raymond coming out of the house, and they walked together to the stables to unhitch the horse. As they neared the building, raised voices could be heard. Algie had a sudden deep fear in the pit of his stomach. He recognized the voices. Sphiwe and Angela!

Algie, followed by Uncle Raymond, traced the sounds to the shed behind the stables. Algie was shocked by what he saw. In the far corner was Sphiwe, wedged up against the wall and pleading with Angela to leave him alone. Angela was thrusting her body against him saying "Kiss me,

Sphiwe. Do what I tell you!" with such venom in her voice. Hearing the sound behind her, Angela turned and, in a flash, sank to the floor, sobbing.

"Oh, Uncle Raymond", she cried as she saw him enter the shed. "Sphiwe was trying to make me kiss him."

Algie gasped in disbelief. Surely, she couldn't expect anyone to believe her! Algie, with his quick temper, shouted, "What a lying bitch you are."

The thunderous roar that came from Uncle Raymond stopped any further conversation. All he had seen was a sobbing Angela and all he heard were the accusations she made. Algie couldn't believe his ears when Uncle Raymond's words tumbled into his understanding.

"I'll kill you, you worthless black bastard! How dare you lay your hands on a white girl." In his rage, Uncle Raymond's eyes searched the shed for a suitable weapon. A heavy spade stood against the wall. He made a lunge towards it.

Sphiwe stood frozen in the corner, but Algie summed up the situation. He knew that there would be no stopping his Uncle in his rage. He shouted, "Run," and when Sphiwe didn't respond, "Run, Sphiwe, or you will be killed!"

This galvanised Sphiwe and he ran towards the door. Uncle Raymond was already back, armed with the spade. Algie saw that Sphiwe wouldn't get through the door in time. Without thinking he placed himself between his uncle and the door, allowing Sphiwe to escape. Uncle Raymond had already lifted the spade in readiness for the blow. Seeing Algie in his path instead, he only managed to lessen his blow, not stop it. Algie was able to step aside somewhat, but the blow struck him heavily on the shoulder. Uncle Raymond's momentary concern for Algie gave Sphiwe a further few seconds to make his escape.

Seeing that Sphiwe had fled, Uncle Raymond turned his attention to Angela.

Spurred by what he knew would be a violent reaction to this incident, Algie stumbled to the door. Suddenly, the words spoken by Lo Lindi came back to him.

He shouted to the fleeing Sphiwe "It is the white danger. Your heart is pure. The darkness of the eye will shelter you."

Sphiwe stopped in his tracks as the words penetrated his frightened, bewildered mind. Then, raising his clenched fist in a gesture of understanding – and farewell – he changed direction and sped toward the eye of the elephant.

"Run on swift feet, my friend," whispered Algie.

By the time Uncle Raymond reached the door, supporting a weeping Angela, Sphiwe was out of sight.

No one believed Algie's version of the incident. Even Maud failed to support Algie. How could her sister do such a thing? Vuyo was summonsed and told to bring his son before the Nkosi. A search of the farm and surrounding areas yielded no sign of Sphiwe. Algie was questioned at length, but refused to co-operate, steadfastly proclaiming Sphiwe's innocence.

Maud and Angela left the next day.

Despite the best efforts of Uncle Raymond, the local police and Vuyo's many sources, no trace could be found of Sphiwe. It was as if he had disappeared into thin air.

But often Algie found himself looking towards the mountain and, particularly when the eye of the elephant was prominent, sent silent greetings to his friend. He knew he was safe.

Chapter 8

Algie had often been in trouble, but this was different. Never before had he felt so rejected and lonely.

Uncle Raymond had flown into a terrible rage when Algie refused to join the search for Sphiwe, and the two were not on speaking terms. To Fanny it was the last straw. What had turned her once beloved son into this bullying, disrespectful and lying stranger? Evelyn and Doris were bewildered – but convention decreed that they take the side of their mother and uncle. Gerald for once seemed to side with Algie – but no one thought to ask for his opinion or if he knew anything that might lend credence to Algie's opinion, so he kept quiet. He had often followed Angela when she sought out Sphiwe. The incident in the stables had not been the first when Sphiwe was forced to run away from Angela's unwanted and dangerous attentions. But Algie's disgrace had made Aunt Fanny even more attentive to him, so Gerald remained silent.

Despite his injured shoulder, Algie threw himself into work on the farm, toiling long, back-breaking hours to shut out the sadness. Not only was he alienated from his family, but his friend had gone as well.

Even the farm workers, with whom he had always had a good relationship avoided him. When Algie had gone to see Vuyo to assure him that

Sphiwe was innocent, he had found himself unwelcome.

"My son has brought shame on my family," Vuyo looked like a broken man.

Algie protested, but Vuyo had said, "Sphiwe, seeing the ways of the white man, wanted those things for himself." And almost accusingly, "You made him too welcome in your world." Then with sorrow in his voice, "The heartache of returning to his place as a black man was swifter and more deeply hurtful than for most of us."

The words, as they sank in, made Algie think for the first time about the emotional issues in this white/black division of roles. He realised that Vuyo had most probably once been the companion to a white boy, living for a while on the edge of the privileged life, only to be thrown back into the life of few choices once he was no longer needed.

Algie could find nothing else to say, so slowly and dejectedly started to walk away. Then he remembered he could say something that might help. "Vuyo, believe me when I tell you that Sphiwe will not be found. He is in the safe hands of someone who knew he was coming and will care for him."

Vuyo raised his face and a little smile touched his mouth, "I believe you, Kosazane. That is what the bones have told us."

I should have known that the local witchdoctor had been consulted, thought Algie.

Once the sun set, time hung heavily over Algie. The evening meal was eaten in near silence, after which Algie went to his bedroom. From the sitting room he could hear tunes being played on the piano. He amused himself by quietly playing the mouth organ he had been given as a Christmas gift by Maud. The return to school was only a few days away. Even though this would be better than the loneliness of the farm, Algie couldn't face going back. His life was in too much turmoil.

He knew what he wanted. To join the army and help fight those blasted Germans! But how? His sixteenth birthday was only a month away, but recruits had to be 18. He racked his brain for a solution, and slowly one started to form in his mind. He decided to try it.

The day before he and Doris were due to return to school, Algie put his plan into action. Uncle Raymond and Gerald had ridden off to look for some lost cows – Gerald was rapidly replacing Algie as Uncle Raymond's companion. Algie waited until his mother went into her garden as she did most afternoons. It was the time of day when the house was usually empty, the servants enjoying a few hours off before the preparations for the evening meal. Evelyn and Doris usually helped but today, although Doris was at her mother's side, Evelyn was nowhere to be seen.

"Damn, she must be still in the house," cursed Algie. He found he was cursing a lot lately!

What Algie needed to do required an empty house.

Eventually Evelyn appeared at the front door, dutifully tying the ribbons of her large sun hat, the essential adornment to protect the fair skin of ladies from the hot summer sun.

Algie quickly went around the back and entered the house through the kitchen door to avoid being seen. He tiptoed to his mother's bedroom and carefully opened the door. He hadn't been in this room for many years. Algie paused to stroke the beloved face of his father in the portrait that hung against one wall.

"How I wish you were here to help me, Father," Algie spoke the words aloud, and felt tears welling up. Quickly he brushed them away, and forced himself to concentrate on the task he had set himself. It was much harder with his father's eyes seeming to follow him.

He was looking for his birth certificate. He knew his mother kept all their important documents in an intricately carved Indian jewelry box their father had given her. But where was the box? He couldn't see it. He felt panic starting to grip him, but forced himself to think. Where would it be safe? A large oak wardrobe dominated the room, with leadlights fitted into the top of the curved panels that spanned the door. That's it, he thought. I'm sure the box is concealed in the wardrobe.

He turned the ornate key and as he carefully opened it, the door creaked noisily. Suddenly frightened of being caught, he tiptoed to the window – but fortunately he could see all three hats bobbing up between the plants. Returning to the wardrobe, the smell from the camphor blocks generously scattered around caught in his throat, making him cough slightly. On the one side of the wardrobe hung the clothes that were not needed on the farm. As he felt the fine cloth, he remembered his laughing, loving mother wearing the more formal frocks, walking hand in hand with his father on their way to some function or other. It almost made him change his plans. He wished he could believe that by some miracle the happy, loving relationship with his mother could be brought back – despite all that had happened.

But the face of the smirking Gerald kept getting in the way. This gave him the strength to continue the search.

Algie felt rather than saw the intricate carving of the jewelry box as it nestled in the far corner on the bottom shelf. Gingerly he pulled it towards him. It seemed to be resisting his efforts to expose it to the light. Of course, it was locked, but Algie felt sure he would find the key in his mother's dressing table drawer. For as long as he could remember, she had kept it there.

He found the key under a bundle of old photographs. Slowly he flicked through the happy memories of their life while his father was alive. A brief joy filled him. Then, with a deep regretful sigh, he returned to the task at hand.

The contents of the opened jewelry box was like a glimpse into his mother's soul. Here she kept her "treasures". Algie briefly touched the set of soft leather-bound miniature poetry books his father had given her, saw once again the ornate jewelry inherited from their grandmother, his father's military medals, the small round silver container in which a lock of Evelyn's blond baby hair was kept. There was the rather strange handkerchief made, he remembered, by a very young Doris for one of their mother's birthdays – Doris had been so proud of her efforts. He was irritated to see several of Gerald's sketches in the box – even through it had to be admitted that Gerald was a gifted artist. Is there nothing to remind her of me, he wondered? He couldn't find anything. Well, perhaps, it was better that way.

"At least my mother has pictures to remind her of me when I was younger, and life was so much happier," Algie consoled himself.

He soon located the neatly stacked pile of folded documents. Slowly opening each one to find what he was looking for took an effort on his part, for he felt he was running out of time. But he forced himself to be careful with the well-worn pieces of paper.

Algie's heart skipped a beat as he saw his name, written in the copybook style by one trained to issue such documents. He carefully placed it in his pocket. He did his best to put all the documents back as he had found them but, not being naturally neat, it wasn't perfect. Replacing both key and the jewelry box where he had found them, he made his escape from his mother's room.

Algie's next task was even more difficult. In the dining room he raised the roller top of his uncle's large desk. Taking his birth certificate out of his pocket, he attempted to smooth out the folds that were wrinkled into it by the hands of time. He sat down on the old leather chair. Unscrewing the cap of the ink pot, he took some time to choose the pen with the best nib from the pen holder. He felt very anxious, for the success of his whole plan depended on how well he could change – the word "forge" briefly sprang into his thoughts but he quickly brushed it away – the year on his birth certificate.

The task was made even more difficult by the fact that he had been born in 1900 and he needed to change it to 1898. Looking at the numbers he almost lost heart, for it seemed an impossible task. But what other options did he have? Forcing himself to think clearly, he concluded that the 9 could be turned into an eight relatively easily by continuing the loop at the bottom of the 9 until it became an 8. Similarly, the last 0 could be changed into an 8 by making two circles inside the 0. Deciding to take the plunge, he carefully dipped the nib into the ink – and accomplished these tasks in a fairly successful manner. His birth certificate now stated that he had been born in 1808. Algie laughed as he worked out that made him well over a 100 years old!

Changing the remaining 0 into a 9 seemed almost impossible. But the dire need to find a way to escape drove him into giving it a try. He made another two circles inside the 0, turning it into another 8. Using the blade of his pocketknife he scratched away the old ink on the bottom left hand side of the 8. Algie then carefully inked in the new 9.

Even to Algie's uncritical eye, the birth certificate was a bit of a mess. Well, he had done his best. He was now "officially" 18 years old!

After putting everything back in its place and closing the desk, he hastily returned to the fields – very conscious of his birth certificate in the pocket of his trousers.

That evening, as Algie packed his school trunk, there were added items – apart from his birth certificate. He took with him his khaki farm clothes, his sturdy farm boots, his trusty pocket knife (not allowed at school), his new mouth organ, and his father's old regimental hat. He had been given this hat by the Commanding Officer as a "keepsake" at his father's funeral.

Next morning, Algie helped Vuyo hitch the two horses into the cart. Often Uncle Raymond accompanied them to the railway siding, but today Vuyo was given this task. After stilted "good byes" from both his mother and uncle, a half-hearted hug from Evelyn, and a smirking, whispered "Good riddance" from Gerald, Algie climbed up to sit beside Vuyo. A tearful Doris sat in the body of the cart, with only their luggage for company. Evelyn had finished her schooling. She was waiting (and praying) for the safe return of her officer from service overseas, when it had been agreed they would wed.

Doris always cried for the first few miles as she left the farm, but her sorrow soon changed to excitement as they neared the rudimentary siding at which the mail train stopped – when requested to do so! She enjoyed the train journey and, as they chugged along, was cheered by the prospect of seeing her friends again.

Once the train reached the Pietermaritzburg station, there was the usual buzz and chaos. The long-suffering teachers, given the unenviable task of "leading the lambs to slaughter" as it was generally known, stood behind noticeboards displaying the name of their school. The boys laughingly fought their way to line up behind the noticeboards – the "ladies" giggling or squealing as they tried to reach their allocated points amidst the turmoil. And all under the beady eye of the irate station master, who was forever promising other passengers that he would find a way to streamline the disembarking process – next time! Somehow, all the students seemed to get to their allocated schools.

On Saturdays, the senior students from most of the boarding schools could go into town for a few hours. Now, on Saturdays, Algie slipped away from his friends and spent the time observing the recruiting process at the army barracks, a few miles outside the town. He noted how the "prospects" lined up – often for several hours – as they filled in forms and the recruiting clerk checked their papers. Two years into the war the outcome looked bleak for the British, her population whittled down and weary from a campaign that dragged on and on. More and more minions on the far-flung satellites of the British Empire were being called upon to come to the aid of the "Mother Empress". Many responded.

The prospects who survived the initial grilling of the recruiting clerk went through the guarded gates into the barracks, and Algie couldn't see what happened there. However, as the "rejects" came out, he plucked up the courage to ask them what had happened. Most of them wouldn't talk about it, but from some he gleaned such information as "failed the medical" ... "fell off the horse" ... and "couldn't shoot the rifles". Algie felt confident he could handle these tests, if he could get past the recruiting officer. The one bit of disconcerting information he gleaned was that the recruits spent two weeks training at the Pietermaritzburg barracks. He now had a further problem. How could he absent himself from school for two weeks before his mother and uncle were contacted and told of his absence?

As his birthday drew near, Algie was on tenterhooks. Both his school work and his cricketing skills suffered – he was even less attentive in class and had been bowled out for a "duck" on two occasions! Each day he feared a summons from the headmaster, demanding he explain to his mother why his birth certificate was missing. And his thoughts were preoccupied as he racked his brain to think of a way to "disappear" for at least two weeks.

Desperation brings a need for innovative thinking, and at last Algie came up with an idea – but he needed an ally. There was only one person who might agree to help him, and that was Maud.

So, the next Saturday Algie hung around outside St Mary's. At last Maud came out with a group of her friends. Algie called to her. Startled at Algie's unexpected appearance, the memories of their parting made her hesitate and she almost turned away. But their friendship went back too far for her to ignore him – and she had immediately noticed how sad and dejected he looked.

Excusing herself from her friends, she went to where Algie was almost hidden behind a big oak tree.

"Please, Maud, can I talk to you for a minute? I really need your help." The tone of his pleading made it impossible for Maud to reject his request.

"What is it, Algie?" she asked in a reserved, neutral voice – neither encouraging nor obviously discouraging.

"I have something to tell you. Can we go to the park and talk about it?"

Again, Maud hesitated. Then she turned away and went back to her friends. Algie watched her go with a sinking heart. His last hope was gone. But Maud was explaining to her friends that she would join them later. Algie's spirits soared as Maud returned to him.

"Come," said Maud, and led the way to the park, choosing a shady bench to sit on and motioning Algie to join her.

They sat in silence for a while, each with sadness in their hearts contemplating the tragic events that had caused such a rift in their special friendship.

Pulling herself together, Maud asked, "What do you want to tell me, Algie?"

Maud was horrified when she heard what Algie proposed to do. But nothing she could say would change his mind. At last she realised that perhaps it was the best solution in the circumstances, but hesitated to agree to what Algie had asked her to do.

"I need someone to telephone the school and inform them that Uncle Raymond has had an accident and is not able to run the farm at present. Tell them that I must go home for a few weeks to help. The only person the school would accept such a call from is my mother, so you must pretend to be her."

"Algie," Maud couldn't keep the emotion out of her voice, "What if I agree to help you and ... and ... " Maud couldn't bring herself to put the thoughts into words.

"And I'm killed in action?" Algie helped her out.

"Yes," Maud's affirmation was almost inaudible.

"Then I'll be a hero," Algie replied, laughingly.

That brought a quick retort of "Don't be so silly," from Maud.

At last, when all the arguments did not seem to be getting him anywhere, Algie said, "Maud, I'm going to join up anyway. If you don't help me I'll find another way. I just think that I will have a better chance of getting a good posting if I go through the Pietermaritzburg barracks – perhaps some of these men will remember my father."

Maud could argue no more, "I'll do it," she agreed.

A load fell from Algie's shoulders, and he leaned over and kissed Maud on the cheek. "Thank you so much."

They spent a long time going over the timing and details of the telephone call. With regard to timing, the best they could agree on was that Maud would make the call as soon as the opportunity arose after Algie's birthday.

Maud was tearful as they parted. Would they ever meet again? "Goodbye, Algie. God go with you."

As Maul walked away, Algie called after her, "I've always loved you, Maud, and I always will. Till we meet again." And turned and ran away before she could reply.

Algie's birthday came – and went.

Each day he waited to be summoned but nothing happened. He began to think that Maud had let him down and he was seriously contemplating just running away to Johannesburg or Durban, where there were sure to be recruiting offices. But he knew that his best option was here in Pietermaritzburg, so decided to wait another week – or maybe even two.

The call came when he least expected it. One Wednesday morning – he wondered how Maud had managed to phone on a Wednesday morning – Algie was summoned to the Headmaster's office. He went with great trepidation because either the plan had worked, or he had been caught out! Which was it?

"Peddie," the Headmaster always called the boys by their surname. "Your uncle has had an accident and you are to return to your farm to assist."

Relief flooded through Algie, but he remembered to ask, "Is my Uncle seriously injured, Headmaster?"

"Appears not," was the reply, "Just immobile." This is what Maud and Algie had agreed on.

"You are to leave on tomorrow morning's train. I will arrange a ride for you to the station. Your mother has asked that I give you all the pocket money for the term to take home with you. This will cover the train ticket." Pocket money was dealt out each Saturday to the boys in small amounts spread over the term.

"Thank you, Headmaster." Algie could hardly contain the elation he felt. His plan had worked – at least so far!

The next morning, Algie – dressed in his school uniform – took only hand luggage. In his small suitcase, he packed the "extras" – and his birth certificate. One of the junior masters had been given the "belittling" duty of accompanying Algie to the station. Algie was able to persuade the master to drop him off at the entrance. But, looking back, Algie saw that the master's conscience had obviously got the better of him and he had followed Algie into the station. Realising that he was being watched, Algie had no option but to go to the ticket office. He had thought this might happen, and so he put his solution into play. He purchased a local ticket to the next station, using up only a few coins. He then waved to the master as he boarded the East Griqualand train, which was already puffing itself up in readiness for the long journey into the hinterland.

Looking out of a window, Algie was frustrated to see that the master had stopped to read something displayed on the newspaper stand. It was almost time for the train to depart, and still the master was engrossed in his reading, but kept on checking to see if the train had departed. Algie had to take a chance. Peering out of the boarding door he waited until the master was not looking and raced across the platform to the washrooms. There he quickly changed from his school uniform into his farm clothes. With a sinking heart, he realised that one detail in his "escape plan" had been overlooked. What should he do with his school clothes, particular the blazer, tie and socks – emblazoned with the tell-tale school colours of yellow and green? He packed the offending items into the suitcase – temporary delaying the decision.

Algie heard the warning whistle of the old steam train, then the build-up of steam and eventually the strained chug chug .,, as the great iron beast took on the task of dragging all those carriages up hills and down dales to deliver the cargo entrusted to it. Algie was disconcerted to feel the soul-wrenching emotions that welled up inside him. Usually the sound of the departing East Griqualand train – taking him home – was the happiest time of the school term. What if he never saw the farm again? No, he wouldn't think like that.

The realisation that he still had a lot to do for his plan to succeed pushed these sad thoughts from his mind. Looking around the corner, he was relieved to see that the master was no longer at the newsstand. Still, he waited, giving the master time to leave the confines of the station. At last he took a deep breath, pulled his regimental hat down to shield his face and strode out of the station. But he still had one loose end to tie up.

Just outside the station entrance he found what he was looking for. A young black man, with a loaded reed-woven basket slung across his shoulder, was standing hesitantly outside.

"Molo, wethu!" This friendly informal greeting coming from a white stranger startled the man, who mumbled a response.

"Have you a long way to go?"

"Ewe," affirmed the man, "I go to my home in Inchanga."

Inchanga was a small town nestling on the edge of the area known as "The Valley of a Thousand Hills", one of the most beautiful regions of Natal. Sculptured through the ages by the Mgeni River as it meanders on its way to the sea, a spectacle of seemingly endless hills delights the eye. Of importance to Algie, it was highly unlikely that anyone should search for him there. He had no connections to Inchanga.

"Will you take the train?" Algie asked.

"It would shorten my journey, Nkosi," replied the man, "but I do not have enough money for the ticket."

"Then I can help you," Algie asserted, "but in return I ask you to do something for me."

The man was immediately suspicious and mumbled, "I do not wish to get into any trouble," as he started to walk away.

Algie was desperate as he shouted after him, "No! Come back! This trouble follows me because I tried to defend my friend, Sphiwe."

The fluency of the white man's Xhosa, something about his manner – and perhaps the possibility of a train ticket – brought the man back.

Algie explained briefly what had happened.

"All I want you to do is to take this old school clothing of mine with you. Give the shirt, trousers and shoes to whoever it fits, but bury the school blazer, socks and tie where no one can find them." Algie had first thought it might be better to burn the identifying articles but couldn't bring himself to make that request. It felt almost as bad as burning the flag of one's country.

After some thought the man replied, "I will do it."

"What is the cost of the ticket?" asked Algie. And the transaction was made.

As he walked away, the man said, "Uhambo lude."

"Yes," agreed Algie. "The journey is long – for both of us. But you know you go to a good place. The road I take is into the unknown."

Thus, Algie had solved a further potential problem.

Knowing that speed was essential if his plan was to work, Algie quickly made his way to the barracks, hoping to avoid being recognised. He needn't had worried, for he soon found himself mingling with many khaki clad men intent on signing their lives away – if necessary – to "serve their country".

Already a long queue was ahead of him, so Algie had to control his impatience and tag along. The progress seemed interminably slow but, on the other hand, Algie felt himself sweating with the heat, and fear of failure, as he came closer to the recruiting clerk's table. Algie was disappointed to see that the clerk was a young man who wouldn't remember his father's regiment.

There was little talk among the prospective recruits. Most, like Algie, seemed to be in a dark place – perhaps remembering loved ones, perhaps fearful of what lay ahead. Were there others whose papers were forged?

Ten to go, then suddenly there was only one ahead of him.

Algie almost panicked and ran away. But he forced himself, when his turn came, to march smartly up to the table and announce, "Algenon Peddie requesting to join the army, sir," he said. He hoped this would impress the clerk.

The clerk concealed a smile. "Fill in the forms, please." was all he said.

Eventually, after scrutinising the forms and the accompanying birth certificate, the clerk asked, "How old are you, boy?"

The question Algie had dreaded.

He forced himself to reply in a convincing voice, "Eighteen, sir."

"This certificate has been altered."

Yes, sir," Algie had rehearsed his reply, "As you can see it was issued in Kokstad. My father told me that they were teaching natives to do the clerical work. What can you expect!" Algie's voice was scornful.

He knew he had judged the clerk well when he heard him mutter, "Bloody savages!" Algie had heard a rumour that native military clerical staff were to be employed and had played upon the concern it caused.

But still the clerk hesitated.

Before him stood a tall, muscular, well-spoken man who looked at least 18 years old. He kept on looking at the birth certificate and back at Algie. Then he made up his mind.

He shouted to one of the guards at the entrance of the barracks, "Give this to the Sergeant Major," and handed the man Algie's birth certificate.

This was standard drill if the clerk was unsure of the information given.

"Stand aside, boy," the clerk ordered Algie, "The Sergeant Major will decide."

With a sinking heart, Algie moved to one side, and the recruiting continued.

Do I cut my losses now, return to school and confess all, Algie wondered? That prospect was even more daunting than waiting for the military man who would decide his fate.

Algie must have waited a good hour before the Sergeant Major appeared. He was a formidable sight. Tall and round, with graying hair, the ruddy nose of a drinking man and a matching beer tummy, his uniform struggled to meet the standard of neatness demanded of soldiers. But Algie saw in his face and eyes a man who had experienced much hardship and seen many horrific sights, and one who still retained a commanding presence.

Algie, remembering the cadet training they had undergone at school, immediately came to attention and saluted the Sergeant Major.

Without saying a word, the Sergeant Major walked around Algie, apparently inspecting every inch of this recruit. It took all Algie's self-control to remain upright and at attention the whole time.

"Where did you get that hat?" was the first question.

"It was given to me at my father's funeral, sir," replied Algie.

Algie had weighed up the advantages and disadvantages of using his father's old military hat to help him in his quest for a way into the army. A little voice inside kept telling him "take the hat", while common sense seemed to point to cutting all traces, including the hat, that might lead to his being caught out. Algie had decided to listen to the "little voice".

"A Cavalry man, I see" commented the Sergeant Major. Then asked, "Are you as good a horseman as your father was?"

"He taught me well, sir," replied Algie, not wanting to appear over-bold.

The next question caused Algie some concern, "In a spot of trouble, are we?"

He really reads people well, thought Algie, before replying honestly, "Yes, sir."

"Anything to be ashamed of?" was the next question.

Algie could reply truthfully, "Definitely not, sir."

The answers appeared to satisfy the Sergeant Major. His eyes seemed to be probing into Algie's soul, but Algie managed to return his gaze with an unwavering determination.

Suddenly, the Sergeant Major turned and commanded, "Follow me, lad."

Algie's spirits lifted as he followed the Sergeant Major into the barracks.

Two weeks later, Algie left Pietermaritzburg to join up with recruits from various other centres on their way to augment the troops fighting the Germans in East Africa. He was now a member of his late father's cavalry regiment.

Chapter 9

A dark shadow hung over Byroncroft.

Raymond was often frustrated with Gerald who connived in many ways to avoid helping around the farm. Fanny had a strange feeling in her heart – a dull ache she knew had a lot to do with the rift between her and her son. Evelyn pined for her officer, particularly as reports of the casualties to the British troops and their allies mounted. Even the songs of the farm workers were muted.

It was some three weeks after Algie's recruitment that the telephone call came from the Headmaster. Fanny answered the call and was confused at the inquiry after Mr. Bryon's health – and even more so when the Headmaster asked when Algie would return to school. Fanny was unable to make sense of the inquiry and all she could do was to tell the Headmaster that her brother would contact him as soon as he returned from the fields.

Piecing together all the information at their disposal, the only conclusion those at the school and those at Byroncroft could reach, was that Algie had run away. But where to? He was too young to have joined the army, so thoughts of the mines around the Johannesburg area looked the most likely. None of Algie's school friends had been part of his elaborate plan – and no one thought to question Maud. The police were approached, and concentrated their efforts around the mines, to no avail. A search of Algie's room had yielded no clues. He had just disappeared.

When Fanny was sad or distressed, she often took out her jewelry box and rekindled the memories that were stored inside. The symbols brought a sense of peace to her life. The Sunday afternoon following the news of Algie's disappearance was such a time. Up till then the work on the farm, together with all they were doing to find Algie, had kept her occupied. But Sunday afternoon was a time of relaxation – and that was when the pain, worry and all the other disturbing thoughts took over.

Pausing in front of the portrait of her late husband, Fanny asked, "Is he safe?" The kind, smiling eyes stared unresponsively back at her.

The first thing Fanny noticed when she opened the middle drawer of her dressing table was that the key to the jewelry box had been moved. She hastened to pull the box out of the wardrobe and, with shaking hands, unlocked it. What would she find? All her jewelry gone? Were the medals still there? She just knew that Algie was the culprit.

She felt relief – and shame – as all her valuables stared back at her. But why then had Algie needed the jewelry box?

Then Fanny noticed that the pile of documents had been tampered with. Carefully, she undid the roughly tied ribbon and searched through the papers, trying to remember everything that should be there. Only after the second search Fanny realised that Algie's birth certificate was missing. What significance did that hold?

She hurried into the sitting room where Raymond was dozing in a chair. It had been a long and difficult week.

"Raymond!" Fanny's shrill call almost caused Raymond to fall off the chair.

"What's wrong, Fanny?" he mumbled sleepily.

"Algie's birth certificate is missing. He went into my jewelry box and took it!"

The implications of this discovery were unclear to Raymond, and didn't really seem to hold any new clues.

"Perhaps he needed it to find work," was Raymond's guess. Boys of 16 – some even younger – were considered old enough to be employed.

But Fanny felt that the missing birth certificate held an important message – but what was it?

Fanny went back to Algie's room and searched more thoroughly. What else was missing? Then she remembered that Algie kept his special possessions in an old tin lunchbox under his bed. What else, apart from the birth certificate, should have been left behind on the farm and not taken to school? She saw immediately that his pocketknife was missing. That was another indication that the disappearance was planned. When Algie first went to boarding school a lot of persuading had been necessary to convince Algie to leave this "part of him" as he called it, behind. Now it was not in the container. Fanny couldn't find his newest possession – the mouth organ given to him by Maud – so assumed that he had taken that as well. Nothing else seemed to be missing. Some old family photographs and the one of his father in full military uniform were still there, together with the odds and ends that Fanny had never been able to understand the value of.

Next, she turned to the clothes closet. Some farm clothes were missing, but that had been expected. Algie wouldn't have got far dressed in his school uniform! She could find no other clues, yet the room seemed to be guarding a secret she should know. As Fanny closed Algie's bedroom door behind her, the feeling that she had missed something important caused her to return to the room. At first, she couldn't find the reason for this intuitive feeling. Then she looked behind the door. The peg, on which usually hung Algie's most prized possessions, stared nakedly back at her. Where was his father's regimental hat?

Feeling weak and confused, Fanny went to sit on Algie's bed. Why had Algie taken the hat? Did this missing item hold the vital information to his whereabouts? Suddenly, she knew. He had enlisted!

Almost in a daze, Fanny left the house through the kitchen door – automatically tying on her large sun hat – and climbed the small hill behind the house from where most of her beloved Byroncroft could be seen. There, under the shade of a lone acacia tree, she sat down and tried to quell her mounting panic.

This was a special place for Fanny. The tranquil vista of gently rolling hills, some cultivated, some under grass, reaching up to the sky. Added to that, the lowing of cattle in the distance, and on the horizon the dominating Elephant's Ear. She hoped that heaven would be like this. Here she could forget the complications people brought to her life, and soak up only the goodness of the land, given by God and nurtured by good farmers. It held both happy and sad memories. Under this tree Charles had proposed to her and she remembered the joy they shared as the tiny diamond ring was placed on her finger. She found herself caressing the ring now, seeking reassurance and strength if her fears were correct. From this vantage point she had come to mourn the passing of her father, and later her mother – but not her husband. For Charles, she had to do her mourning in Kokstad. But having the children helped. She had to put on a brave face for their sake.

As the sun started to set, Raymond realised that Fanny was not in the house, and came looking for her. When he saw her seated under the acacia tree, he hastened to her side, for he knew this would be – in the circumstances – a time of deep sadness.

Raymond sat down next to Fanny, waiting for her to break the silence when she was ready. However. He was startled by her words.

"I know where Algie is," Fanny eventually blurted out. "He has joined the army."

Raymond wanted to scoff at this theory, but had the good sense to ask, "Why do you think that?"

It really wasn't much evidence. A few missing articles. The birth certificate would be a deterrent to being accepted into the army. And how would the regimental hat help?

Raymond, acutely aware of his role in driving Algie to the desperate action of running away, hid his skepticism and offered. "We will go to Pietermaritzburg within the week and make inquiries. I know the Commanding Officer there."

A few days were needed to organise the workload on the farm, but on the following Monday Raymond and Fanny traveled to Pietermaritzburg, leaving a very disgruntled Gerald in the care of Evelyn and Themba. Raymond felt so badly about the whole affair, he was prepared to spend the week trying to find Algie. He didn't believe they would have much luck with the recruiting theory for the boy was obviously not 18 but, to satisfy Fanny, that was their first port of call.

It took almost a day to get through the "military red tape". And it was only when Raymond started name dropping and insisted on seeing his old friend the Commanding Officer that the matter was even addressed.

he Major, after greeting his old friend and being introduced to Fanny, listened patiently to the theory Fanny put forward, and the alternative Raymond hastened to add, speculating that Algie was seeking work on the mines.

"My dear lady," the Major said, somewhat condescendingly, "Boys will be boys. I'm sure your son just wanted to spread his wings a little. Anyway, he can't be in the army. We only take chaps over 18. I'm sure he will be back as soon as he finds how hard it is to eke out a living on the mines."

But Fanny was not so easily placated. "Nevertheless," she insisted firmly, "Could you please check your records?"

More as a token of respect to his friend of many years – not to address Fanny's silly idea – the Major asked in a way that showed his irritation, "What are the boy's Christian names?"

"Algenon Charles," Fanny replied quickly.

The Major scribbled some information on a piece of paper, gave it to his Orderly with instructions to look through the records of recruits for the last six weeks.

While they waited, the Major ordered tea, and he and Raymond took the opportunity to catch up on the years since they last met. Fanny sat in silence. She wanted to know where Algie was, but what if her worst fears were true. Could he even now be facing enemy fire – or injured – or … worse.

At last the Orderly returned and handed the piece of paper back to the Major.

With an "I told you so" smile, the Major reported, "You will be glad to hear that no one by the name of Algenon Charles Byron has enlisted."

"Well, that's a relief, Fanny," Raymond rose and taking Fanny's hand, prepared to depart.

It was only once they had reached the door, and Raymond and the Major were shaking hands, that the words the Major had spoken really sank in.

Fanny, brushing past the Major and Raymond, ran to the desk, snatched up the paper the Orderly had brought back, read it and almost shouted, "You have the wrong name!"

Both Raymond and the Major were shocked by this.

"What do you mean, Madam?" the Major bristled.

"My son is Algenon Charles Peddie – not Byron!" Fanny had only now realised the mistake. Once again, the records were searched, but for Algenon Charles Peddie. This time it was confirmed. A man by that name had been recruited five weeks ago. Reading the report, the Major, white with controlled anger, said, "There is a note that the birth certificate appeared to be altered but as Peddie looked 18 and said he was 18, as well as passing all the tests with flying colours, he was recruited."

And broke the shocked silence that followed by adding, "Please leave the matter in my hands. A full investigation will be launched and I will report back to you as soon as possible."

Raymond rose to take his leave but Fanny remained seated, lost in thought.

Then she asked, "Where is he now?"

The Major, after consulting the report again, replied, "All I can tell you is that he's with a cavalry unit, on his way to East Africa."

At least he's not posted overseas was Fanny's first thought. Knowing he was on the same continent brought some comfort.

"Major," Fanny said hesitatingly as if not really at ease with what she was about to say, "Major ..." and then making up her mind, "I don't want you to pursue the matter."

"What are you saying, Fanny?" Raymond was aghast at what Fanny was implying.

"Madam," the Major was also shocked, "Surely you want your son back?"

"Of course, I want my son back!" Fanny retorted angrily, "But not like this."

Then calming down somewhat, and knowing that the Major – if he was to agree to her request – needed to know some of the background.

Summoning up all her courage, she stifled her misgivings and said,

"Major, my son ... was in a lot of trouble ... he – we – were so unhappy. He must have been desperate to have done this.... convinced this was the best solution." And added as an after-thought, "Perhaps he was correct."

There was a long silence as all three contemplated what had been said.

At last the Major asked, "What do you want me to do, Madam?"

"Nothing." The word was mumbled so softly that neither the Major nor Raymond was sure they had heard correctly.

"What did you say, Fanny?" Raymond needed confirmation.

This time in a louder and firmer voice, Fanny said. "Please, Major, is it possible to let what has been revealed in this office, remain a secret between the three of us?"

The Major thoughtfully considered this request. It would save the army from admitting an embarrassing mistake. With the war going as badly as it was, they really didn't have the time or manpower to launch a search for an errant young boy. On the other hand, was it morally correct to let so young a boy face-up to the horrors of war?

"Raymond," the Major needed more information. "Do you think this lad can handle what he will face up North?"

He didn't need to elaborate. Raymond had been a soldier once.

Raymond was loath to reply but he knew he had no choice. "The boy is brave, loyal, strong, an excellent shot and a good horseman. But if he is ready to face the hardships and the killings – that I do not know." He felt he had to be brutally frank to make sure Fanny knew what she was asking.

After a long silence, the Major suggested, "Madam, Raymond. I think the matter needs further consideration by all of us. Could you come back" glancing down at the diary on his desk, "at say, ten o'clock tomorrow? I think we all need some time to consider the matter."

This was agreed to.

Fanny and Raymond talked long into the night, but nothing could change Fanny's mind. And Raymond had to agree that to bring Algie back with all the unpleasantness and embarrassment that would surround such a return would be traumatic.

Raymond went alone to meet his friend the next day. The matter was laid to rest. As far as the records were concerned, it was noted that Mrs Fanny Peddie and her brother, Mr Raymond Byron had come to inquire after Mrs Peddie's son and were assured that – as far as was known – he was still on active service.

The war dragged on. Union troops took part in confrontations in France, Libya and Egypt. The

German East Africa campaign started in December 1915 and lasted until the 1918 Armistice.

Many died – from bullets, wounds or sickness. Even the loss of a single life was tragic, but the World War 1 battle that remains in the memories of most South Africans is the battle of Delville Wood. In July of 1916, in a far-off French wood, the Union troops were told to hold their position at all costs. For five days the battle raged on – relentlessly. When relief came, of the 121 officers and 3,032 men, only 5 officers and 750 men remained.

Then miraculously the war was over. The 11th day of the 11th month in 1918 brought the Armistice and the surrender of the Germans. In East Africa, the exceptional German commander, General Paul von Lettow-Vorbeck, still undefeated, also surrendered. The ceremony was held on Northern Rhodesian soil.

Evelyn's officer returned and they were married. He had served his country with honour and became a highly placed Commissioner. They lived in "The Residency" nestled into the hill on the outskirts of Kokstad. Evelyn managed the large home, extensive garden and formal official gatherings with grace, dignity and efficiency, aided by many Xhosa servants. Two girls were born of this marriage.

Doris, who followed her sister to St Mary's, married a school teacher and went to live in a small, rural town. Her life was not as glamourous as that of her sister, but she also raised two girls in a happy, loving marriage that lasted almost 60 years.

Chapter 10

The years of war had brought no closure for Algie.

He had been a good soldier, but the hardship and the killings had sickened him. This was aggravated by the suffering of the horses on whose backs they rode into the line of fire. The only good thing to come out of the war for Algie was his interaction with the trackers attached to the Regiment. Although their main duty had been to "smell out the enemy", they also kept the food bags full and warned of dangers brewing when, for instance, a hungry lion or an angry elephant was getting too close. Algie had been amazed by the information the trackers could glean from a lump of dung, an animal print, an indentation in the bush where an animal had rested. These clues also applied to humans, of course. Algie, with his affinity for animals, was a quick learner.

Algie did not immediately return to South Africa after the war ended. His knowledge of tracking procured him a job as a warden in a game reserve and later, with the return of tourists to this animal paradise, a safari guide.

In East Africa, Algie had found a primeval land of animals. The images in the paintings he had loved of wild animals grazing on the vast plains of this complex African continent, he saw now with his own eyes. A return to the beginning of time. A time before humans had brought war and destruction. His favourite animal was the majestic elephant, but the most awe-inspiring sight he witnessed was the annual migration of wildebeest – some said more than a million – accompanied by thousands of zebras, gazelles and other herbivores as they followed their annual migration routes in search of grazing. Covering the vast distance from Tanganyika's Ngorongoro crater via the Serengeti plains to Kenya's Masai Mara, as far as the eye could see the landscape was dotted with animals. But their journey was fraught with danger. The predators, like the German soldiers had done, lurked in the shadows. Lions and cheetahs killed to satisfy their hunger; hyenas and vultures nibbled on the leftovers. The migration route passed through other fearful challenges. There were two crocodile infested rivers to cross. But the promise of the sweet grass that grew on the other side persuaded the migrating animals to launch themselves into the water, praying – or the animal equivalent of prayer – for a safe crossing. The vicious jaws of that river beast who has hardly changed since the beginning of time, snapped and tore apart the hapless victims. But somehow this bloodshed was different from the war. At least the animals did it to satisfy the needs of their bellies, not their egos and love of power.

Never a good correspondent, the few letters Algie wrote during the war years and later from the game parks, had been to Maud. There was still too much hurt to write to his mother or Uncle Raymond. Maud, particularly after learning that the family knew Algie had enlisted, broke down and confessed her part in the plot. She also shared some parts of Algie's infrequent letters with Fanny. It was a comfort to know he was still alive.

Some important messages reached Algie through Maud's letters. One was that her sister, Angela, was now in a "home for unstable people" as Maud put it. She had been caught on several occasions in compromising positions with "natives". Although it was not formally admitted, Maud gave the impression that his mother and Uncle Raymond had softened somewhat in their judgment of Sphiwe. Another was that Uncle Raymond had fallen from his polo pony, injuring his leg, which had required surgery. He would never fully recover his mobility. Gerald was now running the farm, Maud had added. Algie's heart was heavy at this news. I would have done all the work if I had been Uncle Raymond's heir, he thought. He felt anger rise in him at the thought of that lazy, disinterested Gerald inheriting the farm – and most probably letting it go to rack and ruin. Well, he couldn't do anything about it now. Fortunately, Maud had added, the farm seemed to be "running itself".

Maud also relayed that she had been asked to tell Algie that he would be very welcome to visit Byroncroft, but he knew things would never be the same again. He noted that "visit" had been the word used, not "stay".

Regularly, as the years pasted, Algie's longing for his homeland and the need to see his family tugged at his heartstrings. At last he could no longer ignore the tug, so he left East Africa and its primeval herds of animals. But he did not hurry back because he still didn't know what he would do once he got to South Africa. What future did he have? All he could offer was the incomplete education of someone who had left school at 16 to join the army. Or a knowledge and love of the land. Were such attributes marketable? He wasn't very hopeful.

Algie wended his way slowly southwards, stopping for a while when the opportunity arose to do some temporary work or to see some magnificent sight. From the deck of an old steamer carrying mail to the settlements dotted around the shores of Lake Nyasa, he saw the pink veil that drifted skywards and undulated in the air as a myriad of flamingos rose from the lake's edge.

He helped to harvest a tobacco crop in Rhodesia and stood in awe of the Victoria Falls on the Zambesi River. Here the water, called the "Smoke that Thunders" by the locals, cascades some 347 feet into the gorge below and from a distance one could be forgiven for thinking that it's spray was smoke rising.

The year was 1929 when he at last crossed the Limpopo River and set foot in the country of his birth again. Looking back, he couldn't believe that so many years had passed. He had been a boy of 16 with a man's job to do when he left. Now he was returning as a man – but one who was in some ways as lost and unsettled as the boy had been. He knew he was procrastinating, putting off the meeting with his family as he sought ways to slow his journey southwards. He worked for a short while in the Sabie Game Reserve that had been established in 1898 to provide a sanctuary for the rapidly disappearing wild animals in South Africa. From its humble beginnings, this reserve would develop into the Kruger National Park encompassing some 8,000 square miles of land on which protected game could live in their natural habitat.

Meandering southwards once again, Algie paused one day to quench his thirst in the bar of an hotel in the rural town of Lichtenburg. The roughly dressed patrons were speaking Afrikaans and Algie had trouble understanding what was being said – after all he had not heard it spoken since the war years. He did gather that although by now the great diamond rush in this area was over, many of the patrons seated at that dark, dank hotel bar felt that there was still a great fortune hidden in the stony ground.

"Seer's diamond hasn't been found yet!" one of the men remarked, causing a hoot of laughter.

Algie was amused when the bar tender explained to him that a Boer prophet, Seer van

Rensburg, had a vision of a diamond as big as a sheep's head being found in the area.

Algie noticed an old man sitting alone in one of the wooden cubicles and was somehow drawn to him. Did he remind him of his Uncle Raymond? Taking his bottle of beer with him he asked politely, "May I join you?"

"'n Engelsman?" questioned the man.

"Nee, No," laughed Algie, "I'm South African. From East Griqualand. Been out of the country for many years." He was struggling to find the right words in Afrikaans.

"One of the "gentleman farmers" of British descent," said the man in the intonations of an English-speaking South African. "Let us speak in our own tongue. My name is John MacKay."

Algie introduced himself.

"Where have you been?" MacKay asked.

Algie gave a short summary of his war years and the delayed return, then asked, "Are you a prospector?"

"A geologist," came the reply. "I came here in 1926 when the diamond fields were first proclaimed, and have been here ever since."

"Did you find a lot of diamonds?"

It was some time before the man replied, "A few. I thought that being a geologist I would know where to stake my claim, but that was not the case. In the end, it proved to be more luck than scientific knowledge. But it was an exciting time."

A light had come into the old man's eyes, and Algie sensed that he was reliving the experiences.

"Would you tell me about the diamonds of this area? It sounds like an interesting story."

And John McKay, once geologist and prospector – now old, ill and disillusioned – shared his participation in the biggest diamond rush in history.

Chapter 11

"It all started because a farmer was persuaded to build a cattle dip," John McKay settled down to tell what Algie sensed was an exceptional story. And it was.

John Voorendyk, trying to sell his unproductive farm, with his cattle now dying of a strange illness, was persuaded by his son, Koosie, to dig a pit in which to dip his cattle, in the forlorn hope that this might make them well again. As the last hole for the surrounding post was being dug, one of the workers found an unusual stone and brought it to Koosie.

"Pa! 'n Diamant!" shouted Koosie to his father.

Doubting that what his son had found was really a diamond, but aware that these gems had sporadically been found in the area, father and son decided to have it assessed. It was a 3-carat diamond! And so began one of the most unbelievable events in the world history of alluvial diamonds – and all due to the digging of a cattle dip.

The Voorendyks contacted the state geologist and prospector, Dr Harger. After inspecting the area, Harger's opinion was: "There are no diamonds on this farm, a bird must have dropped it here". Nevertheless, the following year (1926) Dr Harger explored the surrounding farms and on Elandsputte

– before he had made his first "wash" – he found a beautiful 6-carat diamond. He set up his camp near a place where a donkey had been buried, and "Donkiegat" (Donkey Hole) become a famous beacon on the diggings. His first wash yielded 21 diamonds, the second 36! The farm was proclaimed as a diamond field in 1926, and once the word reached the outside world, diggers and fortune seekers streamed to the area in their thousands.

Word went out that here you did not even need a shovel and sieve to find diamonds. All you had to do was pull a shrub from the soil and the diamonds would hang from the roots. It may have been an exaggeration, but many diamonds were found just below the topsoil. No wonder people came. In vehicles – shiny or battered, on bicycles or on foot, on horseback, ox wagon or donkey cart – but they came. And a mixed bunch they were. Professional diggers, fortune seekers, the poor and the adventurous. Some traveled from as far afield as Europe and Australia."

The old man broke off his story to take a sip from his tankard and pose a question:

"What is it about a diamond that creates such hysteria?"

McKay had obviously thought long and deeply about this, and answered his own question: "The fact that a diamond is exceptionally hard and can be used commercially as a cutting tool is indisputable. But it's true lure and value lies in its rarity and in its beauty and romanticism. For those who dig the dirt, sift the alluvial soil or scour the coastline for these stones, the adventure is finding a pinpoint of light in a macrocosm of worthless duskiness. The initial seekers who are lucky enough to find a stone of value would not be so well rewarded for their back-breaking work, were it not for the diamond cutters who painstakingly transform the rough stones into resplendent jewels to tempt the romantics. Just think where they are found – set into crowns, adding luster to ornaments, adorning the bodies of the rich and even for the "masses". It has become a symbol of love. Many a poor man finds himself in debt because his waiting wife expects a diamond engagement ring – however small it might be! There is, of course, a shrewd type – those who collect diamonds as an investment."

Algie though about this for a while, then posed a question, "Could it just be a chance to have an adventure?" That's what would appeal to him.

"Perhaps." smiled McKay, and continued the story.

"Within months 100,000 diggers were working the alluvial ground. In March of 1927, 25,000 runners took part in one official claim-pegging race – the largest in history. A 'City of Shacks', a temporary city – called 'Bakerville' – quickly sprung up. At its peak, it had a population of around 150.000 people. Houses and shacks stood cheek to jowl in the streets. In the business centre were as many as 250 diamond buyers (all with their own flags!), as well as hotels, bars, dining halls, bioscopes, cafes, barbers, butcheries, tailors and shoemakers – and even a merry-go-round. There were also 17 schools. The Dutch Reformed Church grew from 8 families to a congregation of 15,000 members. The Elandsputte hospital was built."

McKay paused and seemed to be seeing the city in his mind's eye. Slowly he emptied his glass.

"Let me buy you another beer," Algie offered.

"Yes, please. I would appreciate that," replied McKay.

Once they were both settled, McKay continued.

"It was not only the lucky diggers who prospered, but also the landowners. Some, for instance, made a fortune selling water to meet the needs of the newcomers. Other farmers sold their land or their crops, meat to the butcheries, hides to the tailors and shoemakers."

A sudden thought sprang into Algie's mind: "Did the Voorendyks manage to cure their cattle of the strange illness?"

This stopped McKay in his tracks while he considered the question. "I don't know. No one has ever mentioned the cattle."

Then McKay broke into a peel of laughter.

"A man who cares more about cattle than diamonds," he chortled. "That's a first in my experience. Well, I think you have your priorities right – though few would agree with us."

McKay continued, "At Grasfontein alone, more than 2 million carats were found. By 1927 these diggings delivered more than 79 per cent of Transvaal's alluvial production. But, of course, such a vast amount of diamonds was a threat to the market. So, the big diamond syndicates bought up large quantities of these diamonds, and then let them trickle slowly back onto the world's markets. Diamonds must be valued as a rarity, not a bauble that clings to the roots of a shrub! Within the past two years, there has been a dramatic drop in the viability of the diggings. The claims are becoming worked out, the diamond price has fallen, the depression is increasingly being felt, credit sources have dried up and hiring help is much more expensive. The diggers and the entrepreneurs are off looking for the next pot of gold – or should I say basket of diamonds? Bakerville is disintegrating into a ghost town. Only a few diehards remain. Soon all that will be left are deep holes, gravel heaps and rusting unwanted equipment."

There was a long silence between the two men – both with their own thoughts. One, contemplating a lost opportunity to make a fortune, the other with strangely exciting thoughts welling up.

At last Algie asked, "Do you think there are still diamonds to be found around Bakerville?"

McKay hesitated, then countered, "Why do you ask?"

"Perhaps I would like to try my luck," Algie replied.

"I was afraid you would be thinking along those lines," McKay was frowning. "The last thing I wanted to do is incite diamond fever in another fortune hunter."

Algie laughed, "Well, I'm not looking for a fortune, just a chance to try my hand at something new. An adventure. Of course, I wouldn't mind finding a diamond as big as a sheep's head!" They both chuckled at the idea.

Then McKay ventured. "And another reason to procrastinate your return home?"

"Yes," Algie had to admit, "I'm not ready to face my family yet."

McKay tried to reason with Algie, pointing out all the hardships in the life of a claim digger – living in a tent or cramped shack, the back-breaking work, the "hit or miss" nature of the task.

"You could lose all your savings." was McKay's most impelling argument. He had seen so many broken, destitute men leaving the fields. But then again, he had to admit, there were others who had made their fortunes here.

Algie listened intently to all that McKay had to say, then asked again, "Do you think there are still diamonds to be found here?"

"Well," McKay said resignedly, "You appear to be a sensible, mature man who has experienced much of the cruel world out there. I will give you my opinion – but remember, it is only one old, disillusioned man's opinion!"

McKay admitted that many "boarts" – low class stones, useful only for drilling, polishing and other commercial purposes – were still being found. This was said to be a sign that there are hidden "gems". Some even believe that the main diamond "pipe" was yet to be discovered. And had to admit that every now and then a splendid stone was still being found.

There was a long pause as Algie considered all that he had been told. Although he didn't want to acknowledge it, another chance to slow his return to Byroncroft had presented itself. And, an exciting one at that!

Once McKay accepted that he couldn't dissuade Algie, he assisted him with many of the formalities and necessities. Of course, the most crucial decision was where to "stake his claim".

"I have a suggestion," McKay began hesitatingly, "Every now and then Robert, a black man who helped me on my claim, brings me a good-sized diamond. Of course, he cannot get a license to dig, and I don't ask where he finds it. We share the profits – it gives both of us a bit of money to live on. Robert was always a good worker and very trustworthy. If you employed him to help you, I suggest you also listen to his advice on where to 'sieve the soil'."

A meeting was arranged. McKay, sitting on a bench outside the hotel as Algie and Robert conversed, was struck by the easy way Algie led the conversation, and surprised that they were speaking in Sotho. Algie had picked up a bit of the language spoken by the natives of this area – so different from Xhosa and Zulu – while he was in the game reserve. Soon a deal was struck. Robert would work for Algie.

The "tools of the trade" were easily purchased. Many of the diggers leaving the fields were only too pleased to recoup some of their losses. The old Model T Algie had traveled to Lichtenburg in was sufficient for his needs. He bought two additional items. A very thin, neglected horse he noticed straggling behind the ox wagon of a man obviously headed away from the diggings, and – on McKay's advice – a dog of dubious parentage as a watchdog.

Algie spent the next few days checking the implements, making lists of supplies and "revitalising" the horse and the dog. Fortunately, Robert was a competent horse rider, and before they left the dog and Robert had formed a tentative alliance.

Choosing the claim was more difficult. When Robert was asked for his opinion, he was loath to give it. It took a lot to convince him that he would not be blamed if no diamonds were found. Eventually the three of them agreed on a site – McKay with his geological knowledge, Algie with his "gut feeling" and Robert who had found some stones there. A nearby deserted shack in which they could live was the deciding factor.

So Algie registered his claim, packed the supplies and drove to Bakerville. An excited dog barked from the seat beside him and Robert followed on horseback.

Algie dared to dream as he maneuvered the pot-holed roads. Perhaps here he would find wealth. Then he could buy his own farm. What a wonderful dream!

What he did find in this unlikely place was even more unexpected.

Chapter 12

"Piet-my-vrou, Piet-my-vrou". Algie turned over crossly in his bunk bed. What an annoying sound it was! Looking through the window he could see the red-breasted cuckoo perched in the branches of the willow tree outside – the source of this unwelcome morning wake-up call. Whereas he found most bird calls pleasant, this bird was the exception. The Afrikaans speaking people had named the bird "Piet-my-vrou" – meaning "Peter my wife". It was as close a description of the sound that one could get, he thought – but how annoying it was in the gray light of an early morning.

What a contrast to the gentle sounds of the Makulu doves that woke you on Byroncroft. Why was he thinking more and more of the farm these days? Was it time to go home?

Algie had been digging for almost a year now. He enjoyed the hard work, the simple life, the exultation and disappointments that each day brought. There had been many days – sometimes weeks – of disappointment and then the heart stopping moment when peeping out of the damp earth in the sieve, a diamond! Most were small ones, but two had been of a reasonably good size (well below a sheep's head!) but his bank balance was climbing slowly – even if it was in peaks and valleys and not a more comfortable gently rising pathway.

In the evenings, Algie, Robert and Billy, the dog, would eat around an open fire when the weather permitted. eHashe, the horse, grazed contentedly in the background. Algie had at last agreed to Robert's choice of the name Billy for the dog. Robert insisted that he looked more like a goat than a dog, and Algie had to agree that with his ability to eat anything and the habit he had of butting Robert from behind, the name had merit! As their interaction slowly developed into one of trust and companionship, Algie and Robert shared their life stories to some degree.

Robert's father had worked on one of the farms in the area, but when agriculture was sacrificed to excavation, his family had been forced to find other work.

"My father died of a broken heart," Robert told Algie. "He could not watch the earth suffer such pain as its heart was ripped out and the scars left open to the sky."

Algie had not thought of the diggings from this point of view. As he surveyed the land around him, he contrasted it to fields of pasture on which cattle grazed or mielies stood tall and strong. It did look desecrated with its barren, stony, gravel heaps and holes. He had a sudden thought. If God had embedded the gems and metals into the earth at the time of Creation, were they ever meant to be found? To be so sought after and precious? And at the expense of food sources? Not being of a philosophical nature, Algie did not attempt to answer these questions.

"Do you feel the same way?" he asked Robert.

Robert replied truthfully, "It is hard to feel for the earth when your belly is empty" Then he added, "After some bad times, I went to work for Baas McKay. He was a good man. You, too, are a good man. Many black men are not so lucky."

Algie had noticed how badly treated many of the black men employed on the diggings were. But they stayed because there were no other options.

On Sundays, Algie often rode eHashe just for the exercise. He always made sure he had his rifle with him on these jaunts. eHashe was very different to the "nag" Algie had bought. Good food, regular grooming and a caring owner had brought about amazing changes. A beautiful bay gelding with a long mane and proudly swishing tail. Algie guessed he must at one stage have been a circus horse, for he quickly learned a trick or two.

On a Sunday afternoon in June of 1931, Algie and eHashe set out as usual. Little did Algie know that by the time he returned home, on this bright, bracing winter's day, his whole world would have been turned upside down!

Algie decided to try a new route that day. It would take him through a part of Bakerville he had never visited before. There was a small rise in front of him, and he heard a dog barking. As he crested the rise an amazing sight met his eyes. A young white girl was standing up against a tree with a dog obviously guarding her. Two men were closing in on her from different directions.

Algie immediately summed up the situation. He drew the rifle from its holder behind his saddle and shouted a warning "Voetsak!" (Go away)

He spurred his horse into a canter and placed himself between the girl and the attackers. Seeing the gun, the two men took fright and streaked away, hoping to put as much distance as possible between themselves and the unexpected horseman.

Algie followed them for a short way, but soon returned to the "damsel in distress".

In the years that followed, while other memories may have faded, this day never had. Standing before him was the most beautiful girl he had ever seen. Even the coarse clothing and "Veldskoene" she wore on her feet, could not diminish the pretty picture. A beautiful face, with auburn curls peeping from under her sun hat and – even in this time of distress – a proud, upright stance. She had introduced herself as "Ella Gladstone". Algie was immediately aware of how well-spoken she was – something he hadn't expected in that place, and even more intrigued to learn that she was a New Zealander. Algie was disappointed that so special a girl had been called "Ella". To lighten the moment, he had introduced "eHashe" who bowed to Algie's command. Ella had warned him that her dog, Cullie, who had attempted to protect her, was prone to attack strangers. But Algie had made friends with him. There had been an immediate bonding between Algie and Ella, a feeling of trust. She had agreed to let him accompany her home.

And, as they traversed the broken landscape, they talked. Two lonely people brought together by a collision of time, place and unexpected circumstances.

To Algie it was "fate". To Ella it was a dream come true. She coped with her unhappy life by living in a dream world. Algie was her "Prince on a splendid stallion, speeding across the desert to save her from a wicked Sheik who had kidnapped her". Being a practical man, he couldn't understand how he compared to a Prince, his horse to a splendid stallion, or to being in a desert. What an imagination she had!

When Algie mentioned that he was thinking of leaving his claim to find a more stable job "down South", Ella had blurted out that she wished her Uncle would leave the diggings. Pasting together the disjointed pieces that Ella offered, he gathered that Ella lived with her Aunt Addie and Uncle Joop. They had brought her with them, from New Zealand, to look after their two children, now at boarding school, when Uncle Joop "followed his dream" of making a fortune in Bakerville.

Algie was overjoyed when she agreed to see him the next Sunday.

Chapter 13

Ella and Algie met secretly most Sundays.

Ella had asked to stay at home when her Aunt and Uncle undertook the Sunday trips to the boarding school in Pretoria to visit their children. Joop was not easily persuaded but at last agreed. The vibrant, optimistic gentleman adventurer – who believed he would find his "Cullinan" here – had disintegrated into a broken, desperate, unkempt man – but one who still clung to his dream.

If the weather was good, Algie and Ella would ride out – Ella sharing the saddle, and Cullie excitedly bounding alongside. Usually they followed the road as it twisted and turned away from the land scared by the diamond diggers, into the comparative tranquility of the cultivated farmlands. They would picnic at a suitable spot. Algie always brought special treats, riding many miles on the Saturday to procure them. These always included a big bone for Cullie. Algie, entertained Ella by playing his mouth organ, was reminded of the farm picnics. On one of these picnics Ella took a puff of her first cigarette – teasing Algie by mimicking his smoking habit. On subsequent picnics, she took more and more puffs. Fortunately, she had no access to cigarettes at home. Uncle Joop, she told Algie, now smoked a smelly pipe – she wasn't sure where the tobacco came from, but it smelt dreadful.

On these outings they exchanged their life stories. Ella and Algie had a lot in common, but were also very different. Both hailed from farming stock, but Ella did not love the land the way Algie did. He learned that she was an orphan, brought up by her mother's family. She had been much happier at the Convent boarding school, a fact that took Algie a long time to understand. Ella was a dreamer – Algie lived in the present. But gradually as the weeks went by, a close relationship developed.

One day when they had stayed in the shack as a storm was brewing, Ella had suddenly burst out laughing, but it was not a happy laugh.

In a concerned voice, Algie asked "What is it, Ella?"

"I was comparing this shack to the beautiful villa my aunt and uncle owned in Christchurch."

"Is that a town in New Zealand?"

"Yes," replied Ella, "A town of majestic, historical buildings, a cathedral whose bells ring out joyfully, and a tranquil park with a river running through it. On Sunday afternoons, I used to take the children, Rommy and Klaas, to feed the ducks." A lifetime ago, it seemed.

"Rommy and Klaas are unusual names," commented Algie.

"Uncle Joop is Dutch. The children are from his first marriage. He came to Christchurch to open a department store after his wife died. I'm not sure how he came to marry my aunt."

Ella seemed to be walking through the house as she described the opulence of its many rooms.

"We all had such beautiful clothes, even I did after Uncle Joop insisted that I didn't have to wear the nanny uniform Aunt Addie wanted me to. Aunt Addie made me leave the Convent and come with them to look for Uncle Joop's diamond. She needed a nanny for the children."

"Did you want to come?"

She didn't answer for a long time.

"No," she said "I was terrified. I wanted to stay and become a nun. But of course, Aunt Addie was my guardian, so I had to obey her."

Then she added in a strange, almost choked voice, "I have had some wonderful experiences. The boat trip to Cape Town was such fun. Aunt Addie was seasick all the time so stayed in her cabin. I even went to the fancy dress ball with Uncle Joop. He was a pirate and I was Cinderella." Ella blushed at the memory and pretended to cough as she regained her composure. "But once we landed in Cape Town everything went wrong. All except our hand luggage was stolen at the dock, the department store in Christchurch went out of business but Uncle Joop refused to give up his obsession, even though we had hardly any money left. That's how we came to be here. Ella of the Cinders," she said with a strained laugh.

Although he hadn't met them, Algie was already building up a dislike of Uncle Joop and Aunt Addie.

To lighten the mood, Algie suggested, "We will have to find you a Fairy Godmother."

This brought a smile to Ella's lips, but she was trying to solve a disturbing dilemma – did she still love the broken man her uncle had become?

"Our farmhouse was much simpler than your villa," Algie said to break the strained silence, but it was a good home."

"Yes," Ella said in a dramatic voice, "Our lives have disintegrated from princes to paupers, from castles to dungeons."

Algie had to laugh. "It's not as bad as that!"

Algie knew it was time to leave the diggings. He needed to find a reliable source of income. And that meant going down south to the industrial centres – most probably the best opportunities would be in what was called the Witwatersrand, an area rapidly growing around the wealth of gold which lay beneath its surface. But he couldn't bring himself to leave Ella. He wasn't sure how Ella felt about him. Was he just a "diversion" in her unhappy life – or did her feelings for him go deeper than that. How could he tell?

The situation came to a head one Sunday in early September. Ella had obviously been crying and, at first, made excuses not to spend the afternoon with him. He had insisted, and eventually she succumbed to Algie's pleading.

As they walked to the grove of trees where they had first met, Algie suddenly remembered the day he had asked Maud to help him join the army. It seemed a lifetime ago. A naive farm boy of almost sixteen – now a man in his early thirties, still searching for something to fill the void left by his "excommunication".

"They're sending me away!" Ella blurted out suddenly and burst into gasping sobs.

Instinctively, Algie took Ella in his arms and she unresistingly buried her face into the comforting warmth of his jacket. The sobbing eventually stopped, and they both stayed very still, savouring the closeness. Algie, sensing no resistance, gently drew back and with his finger under her chin, slowly lifted Ella's lips to his. Their lips barely touched. Then he kissed her again, this time more firmly. He felt Ella respond. The taste of the salty tears that lingered on her lips and the dampness on her cheeks was a memory he would always associate with their lovemaking.

"I love you, Ella," Algie could no longer hide his feelings.

To Algie's surprise and consternation, Ella immediately freed herself from his embrace and went to sit under a tree. Cullie followed her.

At last words came from Ella, but it was as if she was talking to herself: "What do I know of love?

I had no love from my family, so I compensated by inventing imaginary friends, but I neglected them and they left me. There is the love I feel for the heroes of my dreams, but they disappear when the dream fades. I loved the nuns and the girls at the Convent, but didn't even have a chance to say "Goodbye" to them. The magic of the fancy dress ball on board ship enchanted both my uncle and me, and we kissed. I have loved the handsome husband of my aunt ever since we met. I always wondered what he had seen in my plump, plain aunt. Do I love the man he has become now? Could I love a man whatever happens in his life? The Bible says you marry "for richer, for poorer, in sickness and in health ... till death do us part."

Algie, never good at handling awkward situations, was unsure what to do next. He couldn't walk away and leave Ella unaccompanied, even with the ever-faithful Cullie in attendance.

Then he realised that he didn't know why Ella was being sent away, so he asked for an answer.

Ella, still deep in thought, remained silent.

Algie, for all his 30 years, had little experience with women. Although there had been the occasional attraction, he had never met anyone he wanted to spend the rest of his life with. The only two women for whom he felt any love were his mother and Maud – and perhaps in a brotherly way Evelyn and Doris. Until now. The feelings he had for Ella were so new and wonderful, all consuming. He wanted more than anything to be her protector. She was like an innocent child, full of life and fun despite her circumstances and surroundings. Until today.

Algie suddenly realised that there was an important fact he didn't know. "How old are you, Ella?"

Ella answered almost automatically, "Twenty-one in a week's time."

Unable to hold back any longer, Algie knelt in front of Ella and taking her face gently in his hands, lifted it until she was forced to look into his eyes.

"Listen to me, Ella," he said. "There is something I have to tell you."

His tone was so forceful, yet sad, that Ella asked, "What is it, Algie?"

Never one to beat about the bush, Algie blurted out, "I must leave here soon, Ella. My claim is worked out."

"I know you want to leave," Ella acknowledged, and added "I'm also going away." Ella freed her face from Algie's hands and hid it in the folds of her skirt as the tears welled up again.

"Has your Uncle come to his senses at last?" asked Algie.

"No," Ella replied, "Aunt Addie has found work for me as a nanny to a family in Pretoria."

Algie was shocked. He couldn't believe what he was hearing.

"How can they do that?" he spluttered. "A nanny!"

"No, no. It's all right. Really it is. I was never very good at school. I don't have training for anything else. I will be able to send some money back to the diggings so that Uncle Joop can stay a little longer."

Algie, trying hard to control his anger, stood up and walked a few steps away before he asked, "Is that what you want to do, Ella?"

"What choice do I have?" she mumbled.

"Marry me!" Algie blurted it out.

Ella, struggling to come to terms with the "nanny" task forced upon her, didn't really take in what Algie had said.

Algie was desperate to at least get Ella to consider his marriage offer. Confused thoughts flashed through his mind. Ella was a romantic ... loved her dream world ... how would she expect to be proposed to?

Some wild flowers growing near the edge of the grove caught his eye. Ella, hearing footsteps, looked up to see Algie sprinting away from her. Then his words came back to her. "He asked me to marry him," Ella thought in bewilderment. "Now he is running away."

She watched as Algie bent down and picked a bunch of wild Barberton daisies from one of the patches of multi-coloured splendour that dotted the otherwise drab groves.

Slowly, but resolutely, Algie retraced his steps, carefully arranging the flowers into some semblance of a bouquet – and plucking up courage for what he had to do.

Ella watched Algie's progress with trepidation, mixed with anticipation. Algie went down on one knee in front of Ella, gently nudging Callie from his position at her feet. Clearing his throat several times – as Ella looked on hardly able to control her nervous giggles – made perhaps the most important and romantic speech of his life.

"Dear Ella", a pause to boost his confidence, "I love you and have done so ever since we met. You fill my heart with joy every time I see you. You have given my life a purpose and a future to strive for. And you taught me to laugh again." Even Algie couldn't believe he was conjuring up such romantic phrases – but they came from the bottom of his heart. He meant every word.

"Ella, I am not a prince or a sheik or a rich man – and will most probably never be able to give you the luxurious life you deserve, but I will always love and protect you."

Then with great emotion, "Ella, will you marry me?" and offered her the flowers.

Ella took the flowers, but did not immediately answer. She sat lost in thought.

If the long and perplexing adventure from New Zealand to South Africa in search of a "Cullinan Diamond" had done nothing else for Ella, it had at least brought some reality into her life. Algie was offering her an escape from a situation that frightened her.

Her long silence, with eyes that looked at him, but didn't seem to see him, made Algie's heart contract with pain. "She doesn't love me!" he thought.

Then Ella said, "Thank you, Algie. The flowers are beautiful." And she caressed the petals, as the silence between them became oppressive.

Algie couldn't tolerate it any longer. He stood up. Turning his back on Ella to hide the pain etched on his face, said. "You don't love me, Ella." It was the statement of a heartbroken man.

"Algie," Ella needed to reassure him, "It's not that I don't love you, I ... I just don't know much about love or what is expected in a marriage."

There and then Algie made up his mind. Even if Ella didn't love him, even if she didn't want to marry him, he had to get her away from her family and their plans to turn her into a "nanny".

"Ella, come away with me, even if you don't love me." Algie's voice was firm and boded no argument. "I won't try to persuade you to marry me, or force myself upon you in any way, but I will not leave you with that family of yours."

Ella stood up and went to stand in front of Algie. Looking deep into Algie's eyes she said, "I know you are an honest, dependable, caring person with whom I have a close friendship. I have shared my dream world and, although you don't understand it, you accepted it. When I told you about my life in New Zealand, to you it had sounded terrible, but you still understand my longing for my homeland. You, in turn, told me why you left home. I am even a bit jealous at the warmth in your voice when you speak about Maud. Perhaps this is a good sign." But she hadn't said she loved him.

Impulsively, she made up her mind, "I will marry you."

At first, Algie was so stunned he didn't know what to do, but as the words tumbled into his understanding he took Ella in his arms and whirled her around in a dance of joy. Both were laughing so much that they almost fell over. Stopping suddenly, Algie's emotions overcame him and he clasped Ella to him, forcing his whole body against hers, feeling her femininity and then kissing her passionately. Ella was alarmed by the intensity of his actions, and she found herself resisting. Algie, once the passion abated, became aware of this, and he loosened his embrace, mumbling, "I'm sorry, Ella. I was just so happy to hear you say you would marry me, I sort of lost control."

"It's all right, Algie," Ella replied shyly, "Perhaps here in the open isn't the best place to kiss so – so – well, you know what I mean."

Algie was relieved to hear that it wasn't his advances that were being rebuffed, but had more to do with the appropriateness of the setting.

But Algie had one other task to perform. He strode to the nearest still-green shrub and cut off a young branch using his pocketknife. Not the one he had left home with – that had long since been replaced by a fancy Swiss-made many faceted one given to him by a tourist after a particularly successful safari. He formed a small circle with a length of the supple tip of the branch, and tied it firmly with one of the leaves.

"Give me your left hand, Ella," Algie commanded, then said apologetically "I don't have a proper ring to give you, but please accept this as a token of our engagement." and placed the circle of green on her ring finger.

Ella was touched by this gesture. She smiled at him and said, "You are a romantic at heart – even if you don't want to admit it."

They slowly walked back to the shack as the sun was starting to set. Both were lost in pleasurable thought, but suddenly Ella stopped and she seemed to have trouble breathing.

"What's the matter, Ella?".

"Algie," she blurted out. "I'm scarred! No man will want to marry me!"

"What do you mean, scarred?" Algie had heard that word used to explain all sorts of bad things women had suffered! Was it of the mind or of the flesh, he wondered.

Dramatically, Ella pulled the scarf from her neck revealing substantial burn marks.

"Oh, is that all," Algie was relieved although he could see that the burns were severe. "I noticed them some time ago. How did it happen?"

Ella replied in a low voice. "My Aunt Gini was angry with me."

"That doesn't answer my question," Algie probed.

Ella was silent for a while and then answered truthfully, "My Aunt Gini never liked me. One day when we were alone in the kitchen she took a cup of boiling water and threw it at me. I was sitting at the time but got such a fright that I stood up. I think that's why the boiling water burnt my neck and not my face."

"But why would she do such a terrible thing?" Algie was appalled.

"She shouted something like 'you don't deserve to be beautiful like your mother' – some words like that." And added as if condoning the action, "My mother died in childbirth. Gini said I killed her."

"I hope she was severely punished."

"Aunt Gini told them I spilled the cup of boiling water on myself."

"And they believed her?"

"Well, yes."

Algie added another injustice to the growing pile of things he was learning about Ella's family.

Algie took Ella's hands. "Darling Ella, your scars don't worry me at all. If you can marry an ugly man like me, how can I let a tiny blemish on my beautiful, beloved fiancé put me off?"

"You're not ugly, Algie," Ella was quick to spring to his defense.

"Well, I guess, 'beauty is in the eye of the beholder' so if you don't think I'm ugly that's all that matters," Algie was teasing again.

But as they neared the shack, Ella started to tremble. This time it was more serious. Algie could sense it.

She was so overcome that she could hardly speak. At last Algie made sense of the words she was uttering.

Ella was saying, "What will Aunt Addie say? And Uncle Joop? They will never let me marry you. They need the money I can earn to keep on working the claim. I owe them so much. I can't just go. What about the children?" Ella was distraught.

"Stop it, Ella," Algie almost shouted, "You don't owe your family anything. Can't you see they have always used you for their own ends, never thinking of you as a person! I hate them – even though I have never met them."

That was too much for Ella, "How can you say that? They could have let me grow up in an orphanage!"

Irrationally, and unthinkingly, Algie retorted, "You might have been better off!"

Ella found that statement intolerable. Taking the symbolic ring from her finger she said, in a most "ladylike" tone, "I thank you, sir, for your proposal but regret I cannot accept your offer of marriage." And ran towards the door of the shack. It was a line straight out of one of her fantasies.

Algie was at once contrite and cursed himself for his quick temper. If only he could control it!

"Ella ... dearest Ella ... I'm so sorry! Please forgive me." He sprinted after her and caught up with her just as she was unlocking the door. He followed her inside regardless of her effort to stop him.

"Please, Ella. Let's talk this over quietly and sensibly. If you really don't want to marry me, I promise I will go away and never come back. But it will break my heart. I cannot let that happen without a fight – I mean, a chance to change your mind."

He was so obviously sincere that Ella relented a little. Still, she remembered that in stories ladies made the men who loved them beg for their favours. This must be what "favours" mean, she thought.

"No, my mind is made up. Your words hurt me too deeply," replied Ella, still wrapped up in her dream world.

Algie contemplated this reply then said, defeatedly, "All right, Ella. If that's your decision, I must accept it." And headed for the door.

"Aren't you going to beg me to change my mind?" Ella was confused and a little concerned.

Now it was Algie's turn to feel confused, "Is that what you want me to do, Ella?"

"Well, yes, I suppose so. That's what men do when they want favours from a lady."

It was then that Algie realised what life with Ella would be like. A need for the romantic ... living with her fantasies ... could he do that? The love he felt for her overcame all his doubts. But he had to be honest with her.

"No, Ella, I will not beg for your hand in marriage, nor for your ... er ... favours," he blushed a bit as he said this. "I only want you to marry me if that is what you want."

This brought Ella back to reality. "I want to marry you, Algie, and leave all this," she waved her hand around the depressive interior of the shack, "But I really don't think Aunt Addie will allow it."

"There are a few ways we can do it." Algie had already been thinking of solutions. "We could elope – isn't that what some of your heroines do?" he teased. "The other option is that we could ask for the blessing of your family. Perhaps for once they will consider your wishes."

"But what if they say no." Ella could see this as an almost certainty.

It was then that Algie offered his trump card. "Ella, you will be 21 in a week's time. After that you don't need permission from your guardians. You can make your own decisions."

"Let's elope." was Ella's first reaction. It sounded so romantic. "What a pity there isn't a high tower from which I could slide down on a golden rope."

But she forced herself to stop daydreaming. "What do you think is best, Algie?"

He was tempted to take the non-confrontational way out and go along with Ella's suggestion to elope. But he wanted to avoid any scandal that such an action might bring. They both had enough baggage on their shoulders.

"I suggest that we wait a week. By then you will be 21. In the meantime, I will make arrangements for the magistrate in Lichtenburg to marry us. Do you have your birth certificate, Ella?" Algie was all fired up.

"It's in Uncle Joop's document box, I think," Ella was having trouble following the plans Algie was making.

"Can you give it to me now? It would speed up the arrangements."

"I should ask Uncle Joop first," Ella said.

Algie was remembering how important it had been for him to have his birth certificate when he wanted to join the army, and the underhand way he had obtained it. Still, the arrangements for the marriage would be almost impossible without proof of Ella's age. What if Ella's family withheld the birth certificate in an attempt to stop their marriage? He was sure they were capable of such an action. And to get a copy of a New Zealand birth certificate would take an awfully long time.

"I think it is important that you give it to me now – if you do want to marry me, that is."

Still, Ella hesitated. It seemed such an invasion of Uncle Joop's privacy to open his document box without his permission.

"Shall I go down on bended knee and beg you to do it, Ella? Would you do it then?" Algie was using all the persuasive arguments he could think of.

"No, no ... I'll do it." Ella went to the corner of the kitchen where the document box was kept in a locked cupboard. When the shack was left unattended, Joop took the keys with him. But as the cupboard was also used to store their food supplies, Joop had left the keys with Ella. She was always careful to put them safely in the pocket of her skirt when she – illegally – left the shack.

She unlocked the cupboard but could not reach the document box kept on the top shelf. It was Algie who reached up and took it down for her. With trembling hands, she opened the box and, sorting through the documents, found her passport, but not her birth certificate. Algie was quick to realise that the passport was a very important document for a foreign resident. He had forgotten about that!

"Don't worry about your birth certificate, Ella. Your passport shows your date of birth. This is all we need."

Opening it to check that all was in order, Algie was at once concerned, "This isn't your passport, Ella. It belongs to someone named "Felicia Mary Gladstone".

Ella smiled shyly, "Those are my real names."

"They are beautiful, Ella ... er ... Felicia. Why don't you use this name?"

"Grandma said it was too grand for me and nicknamed me Ella. Everyone calls me 'Ella'". But then admitted shyly, I'm Felicia, a Flower Child. in my dreams.

Algie was nonplussed but now was not the time to discuss such matters! He was jubilant at having in his hands Ella/Felicia's passport. It seemed to him that at least one of the hurdles in the way of their marriage had been overcome.

It was getting late and almost time for Joop and Addie to return.

After some quick discussion, it was agreed that Algie would use the coming week to see how quickly the marriage could be arranged. He would come the following Saturday afternoon around 3 o'clock to meet the family – and formally ask for Ella's hand in marriage.

"Goodbye, my darling Ella." Algie said as he prepared to leave. "You have made me the happiest man in the world!" Now "he" was quoting clichés!

Just before they opened the door, Algie took Ella in his arms and again kissed her passionately. This time Ella did not resist and allowed herself to feel his maleness and urgings, and did not draw back as his hand cupped her breast. It was the faint sound of an engine that interrupted their embrace. Algie, armed with the passport, hastily took his leave.

Just as he was about to mount his horse, he heard Ella calling to him.

"Wait, Algie, I must give you something," she shouted.

The sound of the approaching vehicle was getting ever closer, as Algie nervously watched the road.

At last Ella came running towards him clutching a box tied with some pretty ribbons.

"Please take this with you. Guard it with your life!" instructed Ella.

"What's inside?" Algie was surprised that such an ordinary looking box should seem so precious.

"It's a secret," replied Ella over her shoulder and she ran back up the path.

There was no time to pursue the matter, so Algie – clutching the mysterious box – nudged eHashe into a brisk trot and disappeared into the protective shadows of a cluster of pine trees.

Algie felt like a knight on a handsome charger as he rode home. The most beautiful maiden in the world had accepted his marriage proposal.

Chapter 14

It was a busy week for Algie. He spent Monday oganising matters around the claim. On the Tuesday – at Robert's insistence – they did their last "wash". Robert had a good feeling, he said. And they found three diamonds, one around 3 carats, and the other two a bit smaller – all good quality. To Algie, this seemed a good omen, but it didn't tempt him to stay. He had found a much better "jewel" to put in his "crown".

Algie couldn't find a buyer for his claim, particularly at such short notice, so he just "packed up" like so many of the prospectors around him. He didn't have to worry about Robert, who had known for some time of Algie's impending departure. Robert had come up with a good plan. Algie had taught him to drive and he now had a legal license. There was no transport for the black people in this area and after conferring with McKay who was able to procure the necessary licenses, Robert had permission to operate a transport service for black people – much needed in these rural areas.

On Wednesday, Algie – and Robert – went vehicle hunting. A married man needed a comfortable mode of transport for himself and his wife. Algie took some time to have a good look at all the vehicles on offer. He traded in the old car – accompanied by a considerable amount of money – for a well maintained secondhand Model A Ford

Sports Coupe, with a rumble seat. Although it was black, it had a certain style about it – a little different from the standard model As. More like a carriage for a princess. Algie was aware that he was letting his commonsense be overridden by his desire to impress his "Princess". He would collect the car on the Friday.

It was more difficult to find a suitable vehicle for Robert. But good luck was hovering over them and, hidden away in one of the yards, they found a discarded ambulance. Its interior was just a bare shell. It had been stripped of all the medical equipment, but its size made it an ideal people carrier. Algie's guess was that it had once been used by the hospital. A lot of alterations were needed, but it would most probably be in good working order within a week or two, the mechanic promised.

McKay agreed to take eHashe and Robert kept Billie.

Early on Thursday morning Algie took two uncut diamonds from his reserves – one quite large and one a little smaller. Both were pure white and valuable. He saddled up eHashe and rode into Lichtenburg. The beautiful face of his bride-to-be filled his thoughts.

He sold the larger diamond for a good price. The diamond merchant, noting the pureness of the large stone, had soon struck a deal once he realised that Algie was aware of it's worth. Armed with a fair amount of money, Algie felt confident that he could breach the barriers that stood between him and his marriage. He was also aware that many necessary arrangements had to be made for such an important milestone in a couple's life.

When Algie wanted to trade his smaller uncut diamond for one of the pretty diamond engagement rings the merchant had on display, he was astounded at the cost of these rings. When asked the size of the ring finger, all Algie could say was "dainty" and hope for the best. In this exchange, the merchant was not so accommodating. He stressed all the costs involved in the cutting of the rough diamonds into the beautifully faceted, sparkling stones that nestled in spindly gold clutches. Algie eventually settled for a band of gold with six small diamonds set into one half of the circle. It wasn't an engagement ring, but it was a beautiful wedding ring.

Algie was disappointed to discover that the magistrate was on one of his circuits to the outlying areas and would only return in about two weeks. But he did glean, from the magistrate's clerk, that Ella's passport and his birth certificate were sufficient evidence for the granting of a marriage license.

He then went to look for a suitable hotel in which he and Ella could spend a night or two once they were married. He felt a thrill run through him as he thought about the honeymoon. There wasn't much choice in the town. Over a simple meal and some beers in one of the local drinking houses, the bartender told him of a guest house, named Rus en Vrede (Rest and Peace), a few miles outside the town. It would be just the place to seal his wedding vows the man said with a knowing wink.

So Algie rode the few miles to inspect the guest house. It was a beautiful September day with the oppressive heat of summer still a few months away. Birds sang in the Karee trees that lined the streets and their chorus continued to follow him as he left the town behind. He spotted some male sakabula birds, their plumage already taking on the black and yellow they use to attract the nondescript brown females in the mating season, their exceptionally long tails streaming behind them.

"Like the sakabula birds," he smiled to himself, "I too, will have to buy myself some better plumage to wear on my wedding day."

The guest house was a pretty place, its structure almost obscured by the many creeping bougainvillea bushes that clung to the walls in hues of pink, orange and purple. The owners were welcoming and friendly, the room for hire was clean and airy, and it had a large double bed! Set in a well-tended garden, there was an area for playing tennis on the lawn and even a gazebo. Algie felt sure that somewhere in Ella's dreams there had been a gazebo. A perfect place for a romantic tryst. So, it was arranged that Algie would let Oom Jan and Tante Sannie (as the owners insisted on being called in the friendly tradition of the older Afrikaans speakers) know when he required the room.

As Algie trotted eHashe back to Lichtenburg, he could see the afternoon spring storm clouds starting to build on the horizon, but there were still a few things to do in the town. A black suit, white shirt, patterned tie, black socks and town shoes were quickly purchased. He also self-consciously let himself be persuaded into buying a few new sets of underclothes. At first, he had rejected the suggestion by the shop assistant that he purchase a new hat, but as he left the store he caught sight of himself in one of the mirrors and realised that his regimental hat really was much the worse for wear. It had become so much a part of him – his good luck charm throughout the war years (even when stuffed into a pocket!), part of his image as a safari guide, and he was wearing it the day he met Ella – that he was loath to acknowledge that it needed replacement. Reluctantly, he re-entered the store and purchased a hat like the well-dressed townsmen wore. It was made of soft gray felt, almost boat-shaped, and the band around the rim had a small feather in it. Once he was a married man, he decided, he would wear the town hat. It would symbolise the change from a drifter into a responsible husband.

Algie purchased a few supplies for the claim, but as he started home, his conscience got the better of him. Ever since he had bought the wedding band and not the engagement ring, a nagging feeling that he had let Ella down kept surfacing. He needed something to replace the silly willow ring he had given her. As well as a gift for her 21st birthday – he had almost forgotten that! But Algie was acutely aware that he needed to be careful with the remaining money from the sale of the large stone.

Then he remembered seeing some trinkets in a shop he had passed, so turned back.

On display were some pretty rings, but Algie's trained eye could see they were made of cut glass. However, the price was affordable so he took some time to inspect the workmanship. The shop assistant, a heavily made-up young woman in a skimpy, low cut dress, having weaned out of Algie the reason for his interest in the rings, suggested that he buy a ring "the same colour as your sweetheart's eyes".

"What colour are they?" the shop assistant persisted.

Algie, the observant hunter and safari guide but not so good with interpersonal relationships – realised that he didn't know for sure. But he couldn't admit that to this somewhat overbearing young woman.

"Blue," Algie replied.

"Then buy her this ring." And the assistant brought out from under the glass counter a large, blue ring in an ornate setting. Algie couldn't image something so showy adorning Ella's hand.

"No, thank you", Algie was quite short in his reply, "I need something more dainty and refined."

"Oh, excuse me," the assistant said in a mocking tone, "Where do you find a dainty and refined woman in this town?"

Algie felt his temper rising, but was saved from having to reply when the store owner, overhearing the conversation and realising that he might lose a sale, took over. He gave Algie much better advice. At last Algie settled on a small blue oval-shaped sapphire ring which caught the sun's rays cheerfully. He also bought a bracelet with pretty blue stones as the birthday present. His gifts were put in appropriate boxes and tied with a coloured ribbon.

The storm was close now. Algie made sure his purchases were well stored in the saddlebags, mounted eHashe, covered himself and the saddlebags with the rain sheet and set off at a fast pace. But the rain caught them a few miles from the claim. Algie led eHashe to a shelter under some overhanging rocks, and here they waited while the torrential rain accompanied by eye-blinding lightning strikes and ear deafening thunder brought its life-giving gift of water to the parched land. The storm lasted, as was its way, for around half an hour. Then the clouds rolled away, the sun came out and, except for the rivulets of water running off the slopes, the swiftly flowing streams and the large puddles in their path, no sign of the storm remained.

Fortunately, man, horse and purchases arrived home safely.

Chapter 15

How the week had flown by! On Friday Algie and Robert drove into Lichtenburg to hand in the old car and take possession of the Coup. It was very different to drive. But after a few false starts and close calls Algie carefully manipulated his new possession out of the town traffic and over the rutted road to the claim. Determined to make a good impression with Ella's family, he purchased a bottle of good brandy for Joop and chocolates for Addie. And a cake for afternoon tea.

But Saturday morning seemed never ending as Algie tried to occupy himself by doing all sorts of tasks. He helped Robert clean and tidy the shack – perhaps Ella would visit him during the next week. He polished the already spic and span Coup. He would invite Ella to come for a drive with him.

He packed all the gifts into the car, checking a few times that he had everything. As two o'clock struck on the old wind-up clock, adorned by a proud German eagle – a trophy from his war years – he could wait no longer.

Algie took the longer route, not wanting to risk a breakdown on the potholed back road. Even then, he still had half an hour to spare, so he stopped outside the dispirited general store cum post office, with its barred windows and front door adorned with heavy locks. Algie was glad to see that the door stood slightly ajar. He needed a cold drink to settle his nerves. Something stronger might have had more effect, but he certainly didn't want to meet Ella's family with alcohol on his breath! This store was one of the few remaining outlets in Bakerville. It now catered more for the needs of the few remaining farmers and the locations where the natives lived, than for diggers. Its owner also supervised the one hand-driven petrol pump situated just outside the store. A blacksmith earned a modest living repairing farm equipment, shoeing horses and attending to the few mechanical needs of the diggers. Across the road was the seedy Bakerville Bar on whose veranda native women and children hung around in the hope of a few coins or some sweets. Algie didn't even want to think about what they might be called upon to do to earn these pittances.

Algie's car was immediately the centre of attraction, with several people outside the general store leaving their seats to gather around the sparkling carriage that didn't need a horse. Algie enjoyed the attention, quite happily answering their questions in the Sotho language, which made him a "brother". He respectfully asked them not to touch the car as it was on show for a special occasion. They were polite enough to comply. Algie bought cold drinks for all the spectators and sitting on a bench – after carefully wiping away any dust or dirt – spent a companionable quarter-hour with his new-found friends.

Algie guessed that Ella had not told her aunt and uncle that he was coming. She would be on tenterhooks. Was she thinking of him as her prince coming to vanquish all the dragons that barred the princess's escape? He hoped he would not be slain in the attempt!

Ella had said that Saturday was usually a good day of the week. Her uncle seemed less depressed. Not having to face the unrewarding claim for a few days offered some respite. Sunday was the best, but they left early to visit the children.

Ella didn't really take much notice as she heard a car's engine come up the road around 3 o'clock. She was expecting the clip, clop of eHashe. It was Cullie's excited barking that alerted all the occupants of the shack.

Addie was looking out of the window and wondering who was visiting them in such a nice car. When Ella went to look, she was so surprised she shouted out, "Its Algie!"

"Whose Algie?" questioned Addie and Joop almost simultaneously.

But Ella had disappeared into her room to change from her working clothes into her finery!

Joop had joined Addie at the window. They were surprised to see the youngish, neatly dressed man burdened down with parcels – open their front gate, to be welcomed with much excitement and hand licking by their vicious watch dog!

It was Ella who opened the door. Come in, Algie," she invited.

Ella closed the door behind an apprehensive Algie and formally, but in a hesitating and nervously high-pitched voice said, "Uncle Joop and Aunt Addie, may I introduce Algenon George Peddie, and unable to hold back, blurted out, "He has asked me to marry him."

Joop and Addie gazed at the couple in stunned, open-mouthed amazement.

Addie was the first to recover. Visions of her pregnant unmarried sister Lily – Ella's mother – welled up in her mind and her anger spilled over.

"You filthy little whore!" she shouted. "That's why you wanted to stay at home on a Sunday. I suppose you're pregnant just like your mother! Couldn't wait to have a man inside of you. Have you no shame?"

Ella started to cry, "No, it's not like that at all." But Addie was not listening and she continued her tirade.

Algie could feel his temper rising, and struggled to control the impulse to lash out at the woman who was degrading his Ella.

` "Stilte!" (Silence). It was Joop's powerful voice that stopped Addie.

"Sit down everyone." Joop's second command, was obeyed by all, with Ella relieving Algie of his parcels and putting them on the table.

Addie started up again, "Joop, I always knew Ella was bad, but I hoped she would change her ways ..."

"Be quiet, woman!" Joop was in no mood for Addie's insinuations.

Turning to Ella, Joop asked, "Are you pregnant, Ella?"

Ella was horrified. "No, of course not, Uncle Joop. Algie has only been inside the shack when it rained, and never in my bedroom. We did nothing wrong."

Addie couldn't help interjecting, "I'm sure that's a lie!"

Joop ignored the remark, and turning to Algie asked, "Why are you here?"

It was Algie's first chance to say anything and he looked Joop straight in the eye and said, "I love Ella very much and have come to ask for her hand in marriage."

Both Joop and Addie were immediately impressed by the cultured tones and intelligent use of words. He was obviously a "gentleman".

"How did you meet?" was Joop's next question.

Ella, who had recovered somewhat under Joop's calming influence and Algie's bold affirmation, smiled through her tears and said, "It was just like one of my dreams, Uncle Joop," and proceeded to tell the story.

Joop only interrupted once, "You left the shack against my instructions?"

"Yes, Uncle Joop." Ella was contrite. Then as if justifying it said, "But Cullie came with me and – look what I found!" She then continued with the story.

Joop sat lost in thought as Ella's excited voice trailed off with the words, "So that's why Algie is here today." There was a deafening silence for some time.

At last Addie couldn't restrain herself any longer, "And I suppose you will tell us that you have never even kissed this man," she scoffed.

It was Algie who answered, "Madam, yes, I have kissed Ella but only after she agreed to marry me."

Joop seemed to have come to a decision.

"Er... I believe Ella calls you Algie, will you come for a walk with me. I want to talk to you alone."

"Yes, sir, I will, but I'm not prepared to leave Ella here to face any more derogatory remarks from her Aunt." Algie was very firm in his reply.

"There will be none." Joop replied.

Turning to Addie he said, "Listen to me, Addie. You are not to say ANYTHING to Ella until we return. Do I have your word?"

Addie started to argue, but with Joop in his seldom used "command mode" she muttered, "Oh, alright!" and flounced into her bedroom.

When the men returned, the table had been set for tea with Algie's cake as the centrepiece. Addie came back into the room looking smug, which did not bode well for a good outcome. Joop sensed that Addie was on the warpath.

Seeing the table set for tea, Joop said, "We will have our tea like civilised people, without any arguments. Please sit down everybody," Joop still had the ability to dominate a room with his presence.

Algie took the opportunity to give his gifts to Joop and Addie, but he kept Ella's presents. He would give them to her in private.

Joop's eyes lit up when he saw the fine brandy he had been given. "I haven't tasted such good brandy for many years, Thank you very much."

Addie took the chocolates with rather bad grace, mumbling her thanks.

"And thank you for the cake, Algie." Ella added, "It's my favourite. Chocolate with cherries."

When Ella had cleared the table, Joop turned to Addie and said, "I have given my blessing to the marriage."

Addie was shocked. "Well, she doesn't have mine, and I do not give her my permission to marry!" then added what she expected to be her trump card. "Tomorrow we are taking her to Pretoria to start her new job. The least Ella can do is to earn some money for us. Repayment for all we have spent on her."

Algie could hold back no longer, "Madam. Ella and I are going to be married -with or without your blessing."

"Don't you take that tone with me, young man. I am her guardian and I will decide what she does." Addie spat out the words.

"No, you will not," Algie could not help feeling great pleasure as he played *his* trump card. "Ella turned 21 on Wednesday, so can make her own decisions."

Addie started to argue, "No she didn't. I would have remembered the day her mother died. It's ... it's ..." then stopped. She had forgotten! But she recovered and repeated, "Even so, Ella cannot marry you. She is to start work tomorrow in Pretoria."

"Yes, I heard." Algie replied scornfully, "As a nanny!"

But Joop intervened, "I want to talk to Addie alone. Ella, take Algie into the garden."

And Ella gratefully ran to Algie, took his hand and led him out of the shack and into the garden.

And in the garden, sitting on an old wooden bench under the shade of a struggling-to-survive flowering orchid tree, Algie dried Ella's tears and told her that everything would be all right. He took the engagement ring from his pocket, knelt in front of Ella and placed it on her finger. The beautiful blue bauble caught the sunlight and sparkled on the long graceful fingers.

Looking into her eyes, Algie was disconcerted to find they were green. He felt a bit embarrassed but Ella seemed to like the blue ring, so he did not confess his lack of observational skills!

Then he gave her the bracelet – her birthday present. She was so excited with the gifts she forgot about the scene in the shack and, unable to stay still, got up and danced around the tree. Cullie followed her, barking in confused enjoyment.

As she came to sit beside Algie again, they heard the raised voices from within the shack. Although the words were not clear, it was obvious that there was disharmony within. It seemed an age until at last Joop appeared on the veranda, and asked them to come in.

"Look at my ring and the bracelet Algie gave me for my birthday. They are so beautiful." Ella couldn't help herself. She had to share her joy with the two people who had been the closest to her for many years.

"Yes, very beautiful," said Joop, resisting the temptation to remark that the stone in the ring was not a diamond. Addie said nothing. She sat in her chair, arms folded, with a scowl on her face.

"Ella" began Joop hesitatingly, "I have to ask you this and I need a totally honest answer. Do you want to marry Algie? You realise it means going down south with him, away from us and the children."

Ella didn't answer at once. She hesitated so long that Algie felt his heart sink. Was she going to say 'no'?

"I don't really want to go away. I will miss you and the children. In fact, I'm a bit afraid. Where will we live?" The last question was directed to Algie.

Although he wanted to reassure her, to make certain she would not change her mind, Algie had to reply honestly, "I'm not sure, Ella. It must be where I can get a good job. Most probably in Johannesburg or one of the surrounding towns. That's where the great gold deposits are and it seems to offer the most opportunities for employment."

"So, you giving up digging for diamonds to go and dig for gold. It will be just the same as this, Ella. You will live in another shack!" Addie said scornfully.

"No. Madam," corrected Algie, "The gold mines are owned by large companies. I am told that they look after their employees well, providing not only a salary but a house."

Addie just snorted in disbelief.

"Ella, you haven't answered my question," Joop probed.

Ella, who had been nervously turning her cherished engagement ring round and round her finger, looked up at the three faces focused on her.

Aunt Addie, who had always been a part of her life. Uncle Joop, the first man she had loved. The faces of the children appeared in her mind's eye but she had grown apart from them now. Then she turned to Algie and could read in his face the longing and despair, as she seemed unsure of her answer.

Not wanting to hurt anyone's feelings, she took the only way out she knew, "My prince has come to claim me, so I cannot refuse him. I have been waiting so long for one of my dreams to come true and now it has. I want to marry you, Algie."

"Then you have our permission ... er .... blessing, Ella" said Joop.

Algie was so overjoyed he rushed to Ella, took her in his arms and in front of a rather embarrassed Joop and a disgusted Addie, kissed her.

Algie went to his grave with the secret pact he had been forced to strike with Joop. In return for the blessing of Joop and Addie which Algie knew Ella desperately longed for – Joop had extorted a sizable amount of money from Algie. It was only fair, Joop had said, as they were giving up the income Ella could have earned.

Well, thought Algie philosophically, in the custom of many African tribes. men pay a "lobolo" for their brides – though usually in the form of cattle. But it had drained his savings considerably.

Chapter 16

The week before the wedding, Algie had come to fetch Ella and driven her into Lichtenburg. He wanted to buy her something special to wear on their wedding day, but after seeing what was on offer, Ella decided to wear her white frock, a remnant of the beautiful wardrobe Joop had bought her when she agreed to come with them on this "adventure". The dress was made of satin and trimmed with fine lace. But Algie was able to buy her other things, like pretty shoes, and a large picture hat trimmed with flowers. And she chose the flowers she wanted in her bouquet, pink roses complimented by the fine green and white trimming called "baby breath". She insisted that Algie have a buttonhole and chose a pink carnation for him. These would be ready for them on their wedding day.

Ella had also asked Algie to return the box she had given him for safekeeping. This time, when he asked what was in it, she replied shyly, "My pretty underwear. They were both a little embarrassed at the revelation.

"But why did you give it to me to keep?"

"I was afraid Aunt Addie wouldn't let me take these things if, ... I mean when, I left. After all, they paid for the clothes. I had vowed to keep this special underwear for my wedding day," Ella explained.

Joop drove Ella and Addie into Lichtenburg on the Friday morning of the wedding day. All Ella's possessions were packed into the small suitcase on the back of the truck. The parting from Cullie had been difficult. He whimpered and whined as they drove away.

It was only after they had been married for several years, that Ella confessed that the wedding ceremony was perhaps the greatest disappointment of her life. In her dreams, marriages took place in great ornate churches, with the bride in a long wedding gown with a train flowing behind her – walking down the aisle on the arm of her guardian, preceded by flower girls and followed by bridesmaids, in gowns that complimented the bride's. The groom, in a highly decorated uniform, or at least in black tie and tails, would be waiting for his bride in front of the alter, with a robed Bishop (or at least a vicar) to perform the ceremony. Stirring organ music would reach up to the intricately carved beams and then descend in all its glory to ripple around the church with breathtaking harmony. The church would be filled with friends and flowers. Even her Aunt Gini had been married in a church, dressed in that beautiful gown of Grandma's. And she had seen somewhat stilted photographs of Aunt Addie's lavish wedding. But there was always one thought to console her. At least she had a man who loved her enough to marry her, unlike her poor forsaken mother.

Ella and Algie's marriage was a muddled memory. A Magistrates Court – dim and ill kept – with an antiseptic smell about it. A constant stream of hapless humanity who had fallen foul of the law passing before them as they waited with other couples in the corridor. Then when it was their turn – entering a stark and uninviting room, standing in front of a large bench, a man in a simple black robe muttered some unintelligible words – she had to be prompted by Algie to reply. Somehow the wedding ring joined the blue engagement ring on her finger. She and Algie signing what she later learned was the marriage register, with Uncle Joop and John McKay as witnesses. Then being ushered out into the dank corridor again. It was all over in a few minutes. Algie's friend offering congratulations. Uncle Joop kissing her. Aunt Addie's stilted "Best wishes". Posing for some photographs.

She remembered Algie saying "How do you do, Mrs Peddie?" and asking him in a dazed voice, "Are we married already?" But the beautiful wedding ring encrusted with the diamond pieces went a long way to soften the disappointment.

The luncheon for the wedding party at Rus en Vrede was a welcome distraction from the shock of the short and impersonal civil ceremony. Even a sulky Addie found the place charming and the welcome of the owners irresistible. Algie had invited a few of his acquaintances. McKay, of course. And Robert lurked in the background. Even

Addie eventually seemed to be enjoying herself. What Ella did remember with joy was the delicately iced wedding cake Algie had ordered. Ella had told him about the treasured flowers she had been given from her Aunt Gini's cake.

Ella was able to drag herself out of her daze to make one joke as she and Algie cut the cake, "At least I won't have to sleep with a piece of wedding cake under my pillow tonight. I know who I am going to marry!" She had done that after her Aunt Gini's wedding. How different that dream had been.

The wedding guests left as the sun started to set. Ella was surprised how easy it was to say goodbye to Aunt Addie and Uncle Joop. Perhaps the welcoming warmth of Rus en Vrede and the stunning garden helped.

Ella was enchanted by their room. It was so long since she had been surrounded by such pretty things. The bed was large and soft, the drapes tasteful. There were pictures of flowers on the walls. The wardrobe had a full-length mirror. Ella was able to see her whole self for the first time in many years. She spent some time twisting and turning, dancing around and generally enjoying her reflection!

Tante Sannie had prepared a small, simple dinner for them, which they ate in the candlelit dining room. After dinner, Algie took Ella to the gazebo and they sat holding hands, listening to the sounds of the night – the croaking of the frogs in the pond nearby, the hooting of an owl, the rustlings in the shrubs.

At last Algie could wait no longer. Tentatively, he asked, "Shall we go to bed, Ella?"

"Yes," Ella replied, "I am tired." They walked slowly back into the house.

It was when Algie followed her into the bedroom, that a look of apprehension clouded Ella's face and she murmured: "This is my wedding night."

Algie had to repeat himself before she realised that he was speaking to her.

"I will undress in the bathroom," he was saying. "That will give you time to get ready." It was perhaps a bad choice of words on Algie's part.

"Yes, ... Yes – that's fine." She stammered.

Algie unpacked a few things and left the room.

In answer to Algie's tentative knock and request to come in, she answered, "Um, yes,"

As he came to stand behind Ella, Algie couldn't take his eyes off the perfect picture he saw in the mirror. She was dressed in a beautiful nightgown which Algie surmised had been hidden in the box she had given him to look after. As she brushed her now unpinned hair, the highlights danced in the reflected light.

"You are so beautiful, Ella," he whispered, kissing the top of her head. He felt her tense. Algie put his things away, lit the small candle next to their bed, turned out the main light and going back to where Ella was sitting, offered her his hand. When Ella did not react, he plucked up courage to ask, "Are you coming to bed, Ella?"

She stood up and went to stand with her back to the closed bedroom door.

"I'm ready now," she said.

Algie was confused, "Ready for what, Ella?"

It was Ella's turn to be confused.

"Aren't you supposed to come and force me to lie down on the bed?"

"Where did you learn that?" Algie was angry, "Is that what happens between your aunt and uncle?"

"I don't know," Ella replied reluctantly, "That's what Connie told me."

"Who is Connie? Algie was getting more and more irritated, but also concerned.

"A girl at school," was the reply.

Summing up all his patience Algie said, "Ella, I will never force you to come to bed with me. I want you to come because you love and trust me."

When there was no reply, he asked tentatively, "Do you love me, Ella?"

"Yes, I think so. and I do really trust you, Algie." Ella stammered, "But I don't know what to do."

Algie turned down the bed covers and slipped between the pure white sheets.

"Come here, Ella," Algie said softly, "Come and let me show you."

With some reluctance, Ella walked to the bed and climbed in beside Algie.

Algie tried to be gentle. The loss of a woman's virginity is not achieved without some force. And the messy semen – spotted with a little of Ella's blood – as Algie, not wanting to risk impregnating Ella too soon withdrew at the last moment, was to Ella so unexpected and obscene that she almost felt sick. One night, several years later – after they both had a little too much to drink – she confessed that on that first night what she did find fascinating was that Algie's soft male parts could fit into his trousers during the day, but grew into this huge iron rod at night!

Algie's most vivid memory of that first night was the reaction he got when he tried to move Ella's legs into a more comfortable position by taking hold of her feet. The involuntary reaction to her oversensitive ticklish feet almost put them both on the floor! But as time went by it was to become a blessing. If he deliberately tickled her feet in their foreplay she became more relaxed and entering her was easier. That, and the tears. He could understand that their first union was painful, but the unexpected tears Ella shed on subsequent nights was baffling.

"Why are you crying, Ella? Did I hurt you?" he would ask.

"No," she would reply, "It's just so … er ... strange … undignified. Unlike what I imagined it in my dreams."

"How did you imagine it would be?" One day, Algie plucked up the courage to ask her.

But Ella didn't have an answer. After much contemplation, she said, "My dreams always seemed to stop before I got to that part."

Algie was not confident that Ella would grow to enjoy this side of marriage.

The days they spent at Rus en Vrede were wonderful. The nights were a challenge. Algie was aware that Ella was "doing her duty" not enjoying the lovemaking.

During the day they enjoyed the many diversions on offer. They played tennis. Algie was surprised and gratified to find that Ella was a competent player, a skill she had learned at the Convent. They walked to the lake. Ella watched as Algie caught some trout which Tante Sannie cooked for their dinner. And often they just sat in companionable silence, both savouring the break from the stress of the diggings and enjoying the beautiful surroundings. Or they talked as they learnt more about each other. Or Algie entertained Ella with catchy tunes on his mouth organ. They both made friends with the two Labrador dogs who, while friendly to welcome guests, never forgot to fulfill their other role of guard dogs when required to do so. Ella discovered to her amazement a tame cat. The only cats on their farm in New Zealand had been those who lived in the barn and whose duty it was to keep the mice away. Tante Sannie's cat was a large sloe eyed, pure white Persian named "Liefie" a majestic beast who ruled supreme mostly from the comfortable cushion on her favourite chair on the sun porch. Ella giggled when Algie explained that the cat's name, translated to Little Darling!"

And Ella insisted on joining Algie when he smoked his cigarettes. She was to remain addicted to this habit all her life.

Tante Sannie was very surprised when on the Sunday afternoon she came upon Ella under the shade of a tree in the garden, with Liefie on her lap.

"You are honoured." said Tante Sannie, Liefie only allows very special people to touch her." It was the start for Ella of a lifelong love of tame cats.

That Sunday evening as they were preparing for their departure "down south" Algie put into words an idea that had been forming in his mind.

"Ella, what would you say if I asked you to come with me to visit my family?"

"When?" she asked, surprised.

"Once I start work I wouldn't get leave for at least a year, so it would be good to visit my family before I commit myself. I want them to meet you." Algie knew this was the right thing to do.

"I don't know, Algie." Ella had come to relate Algie's mother to her Grandma, who she knew hadn't liked her. She was sure Algie's mother would feel the same. "I'm sure they won't like me," she replied fearfully.

Algie laughed, "Ella, they will love you. Everyone will fall under your spell."

Thinking of all those who had not been loving in her life, Ella was not convinced.

"Ella," Algie said, "I have been away from my family and the farm I love since I was 16 years old. I have never felt ready to go back – until now. You have turned my life around. I am no longer a lost, unhappy boy. I am a man with a lovely wife, some money in my pocket, and with hope for a good future, even if it is not on the farm. That doesn't matter anymore. I have you. And with you I now have the courage and determination to face my family and put things right. There is blame on both sides – they should have believed me when I told them Sphiwe did no wrong – but I shouldn't have run away like that, without a word. Please come with me. It will give all of us closure to what was a very traumatic time in our lives."

"I know how important it is to have closure." Ella said hesitantly. "How can I refuse such a heartfelt plea from the Prince who saved me from the deepest dungeon – or at least from becoming a nanny! I will come with you."

Early on the Monday morning, Algie and Ella started out on "Our new life" as Algie called it. The light breeze through which the Coupe cut a path, seemed to blow all doubts away. Ella started to hum some of the catchy tunes Algie had played on his mouth organ. Soon both were singing, with Algie improvising with phrases that made them laugh.

Algie had found his way home.

Printed in Dunstable, United Kingdom

74504847R00097